LAURIE LEE

Legends Within the Dark Realm

Laurie Lee

Be strong and take heart, all you who hope in the Maker.

Book 1: Lights in the Dark

LAURIE LEE

One

Cold, harsh rain pummeled Myrina Jade as she stumbled through the woods. Fear clung to her like a shadow. The heartbeat against her chest slowed. From somewhere close ahead on the left, sheep bleated following a roll of thunder. Myrina closed her eyes. A barn meant possible shelter. Would humans be close as well? Someone to whom she could trust her baby? The infant miraculously clung to life, but for how much longer?

With a sigh, Myrina adjusted her head covering, hiding her pointing ears. Soaked to the skin and shivering, she moved from the relative protection of trees to cross a field. Normally, influencing weather would not have been beyond her capabilities, but for now, her focus remained with the baby. Her baby. An urge to cry swept through her. Strong emotion would not help either of them. Just beyond the barn, she noticed lights from a farmhouse. It was a sprawling building, added to over the years. She breathed. By the Maker, let them take her in. Though the hour was late, someone was up. Myrina banged against the door. A weak cry sounded from her baby as the door opened.

~

Something kept Molly from sleep. The storm outside whistled through the fireplace. She watched flames flicker against the wood logs as she listened for footsteps from the boys' room above. So far, none of them seemed disturbed.

With sleep eluding her, she pulled a knitting project from a basket beside her chair. Duncan grew so quickly, he'd need a new coat for next winter. At first, she thought the pounding came from upstairs, but as she lifted her head, she noticed the noise was behind her. She frowned. Someone was at the door on a night like this? She dropped her knitting, jumped to her feet, and hurried across the room.

The woman she saw was no one she knew. Rain dripped from the navy-blue cloak covering the stranger to her feet. The hair and skin she could see was soaked as well. Something in her eyes reminded Molly of a hunted animal. "Bless the night, what are you doing?" Her thick accent sounded surprised, not harsh.

~

A woman in nightclothes stared at Myrina. The woman had reddish hair swept back into a long braid. Myrina blinked water from her eyes. "I was caught unawares in the storm. My baby is unwell."

"Baby?" The other woman gasped. "What are you doing in this weather with a wee one?" She stepped to the side. "We haven't much, but a warm fire."

Myrina opened her cloak and unwrapped the baby. "Her name is Estellyn. Estellyn Rose." She handed her child to the stranger. "I left supplies in the barn. Hold her close to the fire while I fetch them."

~

Molly took the baby. The child's lips were already turning blue. "You should come in."

"Let me get our things, she will need them."

Molly withheld her protest. The baby released a faint breath. There wouldn't be many more. She nodded, wrapping her arms around her. "Hurry. If the boys were awake, I could send them to fetch."

The pale woman hinted at a smile. "All will be well, as it should be."

Molly sighed. As it should be? She didn't want to feel the death of another child in her arms. She hurried to the fire, standing as close as she dared.

~

Myrina walked away from the house. Through her daughter no longer rested against her chest, she could still feel her heartbeat, a faint, hesitant beat. "Estellyn must live," Myrina whispered as she fell against the side of the barn. Cold seeped into her, but she pushed away the discomfort. She went inside the barn and sat, huddled against a wall. She held her hands above her lap and bent over them. She breathed, in and out. With each release, white fog fell from her. It dripped like dew from her silver hair, like tears from her blue eyes. Her own heartbeat skipped and fell silent.

~

Molly rocked the tiny bundle in her arms as she stood in front of the fire. Estellyn's eyes opened. She stared silently at Molly. Though she was paler than Molly's rugged sons, the blue tinge around the baby's lips faded to a more natural color. Molly frowned. The baby wiggled in her arms, more life-like than she had been. "Is the warmth all you needed?" She glanced at the fire, then moved to her rocking chair. A tiny hand stretched out of the blanket. Molly caught it with a smile. "Your mother will be happy when she returns." She rocked, enjoying the feel of the tight hold the baby had on her. "Estellyn Rose, eh? I wonder where you are from and where you are going. Much too little for travel, poor thing. Your mother must be desperate." She continued to rock her as they waited for the other woman to return.

They fell asleep waiting.

"Mother?" A young boy with a wild head of red hair woke her as he stood beside the chair.

Molly grabbed the baby close to her, both of them startled awake. Estellyn cried, but Molly stretched and looked around. "The other woman? Is there no one else here, Finn?"

Finn stared at the baby. "Is that another brother?"

Molly shook sleep from her head. "It is a girl. She arrived with her mother during the night. The woman went to the barn to fetch their things. I must have fallen asleep."

Finn looked around the room. "There's no one else here, except Lachlan. He just came down the stairs."

"Both of you, go to the barn. See if she is there. Perhaps she has fallen."

But it was worse, much worse. Moments later, as Molly fetched milk for the baby, the boys ran across the garden, screaming.

"Heavens above, what is that racket?" Corman hollered from the stairs. His booted feet sounded like drums as he rushed to the first floor. "What has happened?"

The boys ran inside, going to their father. "She's dead. Lachlan touched her, and she didn't move. He said she felt like ice."

Molly ran into the room. "Dead? No, it cannot be."

Corman stared at the crying baby in her arms. "What is that?"

Molly handed the baby to Finn. "Hold her. Dip your finger in milk so she can drink a little. That will help with the noise." She glanced at Corman. "We must hurry."

There was no point. The woman was dead, as her sons had said. She crouched in front of her, holding her cold hand. "Poor thing. What was so desperate you risked your life and the life of your baby?"

Corman stood with crossed arms nearby. "Who is she? Why is she here?"

Molly wiped a tear from her eye. "She came in the night, desperate for shelter. I held the baby as she ran here to get their things."

He frowned. "I see nothing but her."

Molly shook her head. "I do not understand. I thought the baby but moments from death herself, yet she has lived, and her mother died."

"What are we to do with her?"

"Give her a proper burial. Someone must be missing her somewhere."

"And the baby?"

"She's just a little thing. Keep her until family comes to claim her."

Corman rubbed the back of his neck. "A seventh child is not an easy thing to have."

"She is a girl. If no one comes for her, I will have help in the house. Six sons are a blessing, but they do not help much for me."

Corman stood silent a moment before nodding. "I will have Finn and Morin bring the wagon to carry her to the burying grounds."

~

Molly sighed as she stood close to the dead woman. Duncan ran into the barn with his arms full. Molly motioned to direct him. "Lay the sheet by the doorway."

Corwin wrapped his arms around the dead woman while Molly lifted her feet. They moved her with care onto the sheet. The woman had been tall and extremely thin. As Molly adjusted the cloak to cover the woman, she noticed a necklace. She glanced at Corman. "Should we keep it for the child?"

He shrugged.

Molly sighed. "It may guide her to family someday." If her family had been good, would she run away with a newborn? She sighed again. "I have a box I can put it in."

Corman let her search the body for other items. She wore no other jewelry, and the pockets of the cloak were empty. They both wrapped the sheet around the body and secured it with ties.

Corman waved for his two eldest sons, Finn and Callum. Once they had the wrapped body in the wagon, Finn led the ox while Callum walked beside the wagon to keep it steady. The others followed as they trailed across the field to a burying plot. Duncan handed the baby to Molly, who held her as they settled Estellyn's mother in a deep hole. Corman placed a silver coin on the woman's forehead. They stood a moment then he nodded to Finn and Callum. The boys used shovels to cover her with dirt.

Before the sun reached overhead, Molly stood looking at the burying ground with Duncan at her side. Duncan tilted his head and gazed at the markers which showed where other family members were buried. "We should mark her sleep."

Molly nodded. With the grass returned to its place, there was nothing to indicate someone had been buried. "She called herself Myrina Jade."

He reached for Estellyn's fingers. "Will you tell my sister about her someday?" The baby gurgled, grasping him tightly.

Molly laughed. "She may have family searching for her already."

"We should keep her with us."

Molly glanced at the other markers again, one of which was another son. The new baby in her arms helped heal something of that hurt. "It may not be up to us. We will do what is best for the lass."

Wind blew, and they returned to the farmhouse.

Two

Somewhere high above, where the tree canopy touched the sky, rain fell. Drips slithered their way from the touch of air to the dank, shadowed forest floor below. Estellyn Rose looked up as a thick drop splashed against her shoulder. "This storm does not want to let up. There must be shelter here somewhere," she muttered as she searched the unfamiliar woods. There seemed to be something. She jogged along an ill-kept path. Her leather boots made no sound. Part of the mountain stood on her left. She slipped into a dark patch that cut into the rock. Within moments, water fell like a stream just beyond her shelter. She tugged on her green tunic below the leather belt to fix the shoulder that drooped almost to her elbow.

Air moved around her. It wasn't only from outside of the cave. Air moved from behind, trying to loosen tendrils of her blond hair from its braided coil. She checked behind her, but there was no way to see into the dark. She followed the edge of the cave wall, keeping her fingers in contact with rock, and moved further in. She could still see the green forest beyond the opening. She turned toward the dark and took more steps.

The cave curved. She stubbed her toe on a larger rock in the path but continued. Once she turned the corner, light from the entrance faded away. She stood still for a few moments, letting her eyes adjust. She expected all to be black, but she found she could see her hand on the wall beside her. She wiggled fingers to be certain. *Is the light of day stretching this far?* The cave went further still. Space narrowed and became more like a tunnel. "Fourteen years is old enough to brave the dark," she repeated the words her older brothers used to taunt her. The quiet didn't like the sound of her voice.

Light remained dim, and yet there was light. Somehow. Estellyn heard rumbling noises. She crouched against a slight outcropping in the side of the tunnel. She closed her eyes and listened. At first, the rumbling seemed the only noise. Water going over and around rocks. *Must be from the storm.* There was something else. Softer than moving water. There were thuds, something striking the ground. The sound reminded her of an animal.

Puzzled, she moved quicker, keeping as close to the wall as she could and slightly bent. The tunnel continued for some time, then gradually widened. She stepped into a puddle. She leaned against the wall and water washed over her hand. Rain had found its way through the dirt from above. She could just make out the movement of an underground stream a few more steps in front of her. Beyond that stood a white horse.

Estellyn stared. A horse? This deep in the forest and underground? Had it wandered and gotten stuck? She noticed no one else. The horse jerked its head and pawed at the ground but didn't move far. *Are you chained?* She walked to the edge of the stream that gurgled across rocks. It didn't appear deep, but how could she keep her balance and not stumble into the water? She glanced around but there was nothing. "I came into the cave to stay dry, but I guess a tumble in the water won't hurt too badly," she whispered, her voice carried away with the water.

The horse neighed in response. Estellyn breathed as she stepped into the stream. She could feel movement flowing over her boots. She checked each step, trying not to catch herself on a moving stone. It wasn't until she cleared the other side she fell to her knees in sand. She blinked, keeping crouched on the ground as she wiped her hands on her tunic. There were more tunnels leading further in. She could hear things, or feel them, throbs and drums. "What is this place?"

A soft bray brought her attention back to the horse, a white horse with a mane and tail that flowed longer than her own hair. She stood then stepped nearer. From its forehead rose a horn. Not a curved horn like one of the highland cows her father farmed. This horn stood straight with a point that could impale. As she moved closer, the horse looked at her. Something bound it to a hold in the cave wall. Estellyn quickened her pace. The binding meant someone had been here. She glanced at the tunnels. They could be watching her or on their way. An urge to run back where she had come halted her steps. *Return to safety.* But what about the horse? Trapped in the dark? Nothing to eat or close enough to drink?

Estellyn shook her head even as she frowned. She was not leaving a helpless animal to suffer. She renewed her steps. Heart pounding, she held her hand to allow the horse to sniff. The horn, though straight, did curl around itself and somehow gleamed as though it were more jewel or metal than bone. Her heart lightened when the animal nibbled her fingers. "Got yourself caught?" She whispered, then tugged on the strap holding the horse to the wall.

The knots on either end of the strap didn't budge as Estellyn tried to undo them. She pulled a short dagger from its sheath on her leather belt. "Hopefully, this will be sharp enough." She held the strap with her left hand and pulled as hard as she could from the hold in the wall. She cut back and forth until the leather strap snapped. Estellyn beamed as the horse shook its head and pranced. It went to the water and drank. When it finished, it stood beside Estellyn quivering.

A louder noise sounded through one of the tunnels behind them. Estellyn grabbed onto the horse as her heart thudded. She pushed against it. "You should go." But the animal remained. Estellyn tried again with no result. "Please tell me you aren't afraid of water." The horse shook its head. "Then what?" Was she really talking to a horse? But, before she could chide herself further, the horse knelt its front legs and lowered its head, making it possible for Estellyn to climb onto its back. Another pounding from the deep, and she jumped, ungraceful as only a nonrider can be.

She wrapped her arms around the large neck and tried to grip the body with her legs. The horse stood and she managed not to fall off. It moved forward, into the water, then out the other side. Estellyn buried her face with eyes squeezed shut. Her heart was pounding, but fear of what was coming up the tunnel outweighed her fear of the horse. The air freshened. In minutes, the tunnel opened into the wider cave. When Estellyn looked, light surrounded her. The light in the woods beyond the cave paled in comparison to the gleam of the horse. Estellyn slid to the ground, keeping hold until she was certain her feet weren't going to stumble beneath her. Blue eyes peered at her. "Are you going to be safe? Where will you go?" Instead of an answer, the horse nuzzled her.

Sounds from the deep place were muted, but not silent. "You are welcome to follow me home." Estellyn adjusted her tunic once more then stepped out of the cave. The rain had stopped. She breathed deeply. The horse passed her. "Be careful not to get caught again," she cautioned, then hurried to find the overgrown path she'd used earlier. "Don't want to get myself caught either." Before she let the trees of the woods swallow her up, she gazed back one last time. Too much curiosity could be a dangerous thing. She retraced her steps in the general direction of the midlands and the family farm. It would take her another day to get there. What would they think of the white horse?

~

"How far did you wander this time?"

Estellyn sat beside her mother on a bench by the front door. She swung her legs as she looked at a broken fence in the distance. "Did the storm do that? I didn't mean to be away so long. I tried to get out of the storm's path."

Mother laughed. "You are a wanderer. Still, you are too young to be gone for days."

"I should go with my brothers into the highlands with our sheep."

Mother shook her head. "They would feel responsible for you, splitting their attention from the herds. In a few years, perhaps."

"Have you never wanted to travel? To experience other places in the world?"

Mother shrugged. "I grew up in the midlands. Corman is a good mate. I enjoy my season of rest when they go with the herds into the highlands." She grinned. "My life is good."

Estellyn tilted her head. "Should I want the same as you?"

At that, mother laughed. "The same as me? You're as different as morning is from evening. It's not bad, your life will be different than mine." She stood. "Still, there are skills even a wanderer should know. Like preparing meals."

Estellyn pulled a bag from her pocket. "I brought herbs I found on the way. Will any of them be good for cooking?"

They had just entered the house when two brothers ran in from the back, shouting.

"Lewach and Morin, calm yourselves." Mother crossed her arms as she stared at them.

"Finn and Callum were fighting, and Callum fell onto a rock. His leg busted."

"Mercy save me from foolish boys," mother grumbled as she grabbed a basket with cloth strips. "Use these to bind two sticks to his leg. Get a blanket from his bed. You'll all have to carry him home."

Estellyn watched Lewach and Morin. They weren't really boys, both at least five years her senior. All her brothers looked like father with thick red hair and grayish brown eyes. They grabbed the supplies and ran back the way they'd come.

"Put a waxed sheet on Callum's bed. Find a few sturdy planks we can use to set his leg."

Estellyn did as directed. It was hours later before a team of five brothers made their way across the field and into the garden. Callum's greenish pale skin hinted at his pain. Estellyn prepared a tea with bark to ease his pain and lavender to aid sleep. She hummed as she heated the concoction but could still hear the cries of Callum as they set his leg. His red hair even seemed pale when she finally went to his room. She sat on a stool beside him. "Drink this, it will help." She lifted his head so he could sip without dribbling on his shirt. She pressed a cool towel on his forehead between drinks.

"I'm not fevered," he muttered.

She grinned. "I infused it with lavender to help you sleep."

"I will be in too much pain to sleep."

"Not if you relax your body."

"Did the others return to the highlands?"

"Mother asked them to stay tonight, in case she needs their help." Estellyn helped him with another drink. "Were you and Finn really fighting?"

"Just because he's older, doesn't mean he gets to make all the decisions, ordering us around."

"Father is there, shouldn't he be in charge?"

"With six sons, he doesn't have to continue making the trek into the highlands for the summer. He's training us to take over for him." Callum sighed and settled with his eyes closed. "I think I could take a rest for a little bit."

Estellyn returned to the kitchen. "I'll get more potatoes cut," she said seeing all the others around the table.

Lewach grinned. "If we're all staying for supper, best make another loaf of bread as well."

~

"Must not have been as bad as we all thought," Callum wiggled his toes as he sat up in his bed the next morning.

"Do not move much," Mother admonished. "Those boards are there to set your leg"

"It barely hurts."

She shook her head. "We will wait a few more days and see how it is."

With a sigh, he agreed.

Estellyn stopped at the door. "Good morning, sleepyhead. Do you want another cup of tea today?"

Mother folded her arms. "Not if it's taking too much an edge off his pain and he becomes reckless."

Callum lifted his hands. "I agreed to remain in bed. A cup of tea would be lovely."

Estellyn grinned. "The pigs knocked their pen down. Piglets have run. I'll find them." She handed a mug to mother. "I won't go far, I promise."

The midlands were a mix of farmland, a few grazing fields, and woods. Piglets likely foraged for truffles and mushrooms at the edge of the forest. Estellyn headed in that direction. Standing among the trees reminded Estellyn of the horse. "I hope you found a safe place," she said to no one in particular. Gruntings nearby alerted her to piglets. She found three easily, setting them in her cart with a few tasty treats to keep them occupied. She collected a handful of truffles and put them in her pouch. "Now, where are the others?" The three pigs in the cart blinked innocently. Estellyn crouched on the ground and peered among the trunks and underbrush. She searched farther and farther until she noticed them at a blackberry bush. She shook her head. It would not be easy terrain for the cart. She covered it and secured the three that were already there then went to capture her other pair of runners.

It was further than she first thought. Though she was out of breath by the time she climbed to their location, they still munched happily on ripening blueberries. She grabbed one and then the other up into her arms. "You are fortunate something bigger and hungrier than you hasn't come along already." She returned to the others, set them together, and pulled the wagon back to their pen behind the barn.

Not far beyond the pen was a plot of land completely fenced, where family had been buried. There was a brother she'd never known, a set of grandparents, and one stranger. It was a woman named Myrina Jade. Mother never spoke of her, claiming the time had not yet come. Estellyn felt her fingers tingle as she stared at the simple marker. They were all simple, but this one, for reasons she didn't understand, meant more to her than the others. What did it mean? She rubbed her hands and noticed dirt. With a quick smile for the stranger, she went to wash up.

LAURIE LEE

Three

Deep in the woods, beyond the trails and paths trod by humans, a dark thing lurked. It had come for the unicorn, but the creature was not where it had been left. It shook, anger darkening its visage. Something other than the creature had been in the cave. Following the trail of an unusual scent in the air brought it to the edge of the cave. It hovered in the shadows. There was none of the brightness that drove pain into its head, and yet the light still scraped like a burning stick across its flesh. What hovered in the air promised better than the pain. It stepped from the shelter of the rock into a thicket of trees.

It bent its face toward the ground and sniffed. Animal it knew, large stupid beasts raised in fields until they were slaughtered for flesh and meat. It groped a little further then reared back. Unicorn. The essence of the holy creature burned into the malice that hardened its thoughts and heart. Carefully, it slunk around the cloying purity of the Maker's gift. He sought something else, a different scent both innocent and sweet. His claws dug into the soil when he found a trace. His memory absorbed that smell. He wanted it, like a possession to be consumed. For a moment, he glanced back at the entrance to the Dark Realm. His master would demand it of him, toying with it until sweet turned bitter and rank. There was no pleasure to be had once an innocent had been spoiled.

With claws and face buried in the dirt to engulf the lingering trail left by its prey, it breathed. Its body shook as though a great drug threatened to ravage what little sense remained in his mind. Satisfied and yet thirsting for more, it clambered to the nearest tree to stand. Its vile, twisted shape would fail any attempt it made to find the one who had stolen the unicorn. "Master," the gravelly voice caused a jay to shriek. "Make me as one of them."

Deep within the Dark Realm, something moved. A figure as white as the unicorn sat upon a throne. His hair gleamed silver like mists of the sea, falling down his back. Blackest red robes contrasted with his white skin. His sharply pointed ear twitched at the faint call of a servant. His mind wrapped around the voice. He hissed at a sudden slash of pain. Something absorbed by his servant passed to him. Shards like searing glass scraped across his skin, burning a line from cheek to chest. He leapt to his feet. Goodness drawn from the surface world morphed into a solid jewel. Red veins stood out against his white skin as he scowled. The gem hit the floor by his feet and shone green in the dim light of the Dark Realm.

Morgeth knelt and retrieved it. Across the hall, a hearth burned with black flames from the depths of the world. He tossed in the jewel. It should have sparked and flickered to nothing, but this jewel turned the fire around it green as well, green brightness that hurt to behold. More dark flames reared up from the depths. The green light held its own far too long before it was gobbled up.

Morgeth sneered. "The one my servant seeks will burn in my fire if it has to be taken to the depths of hell. Send him."

Smoke rose from the black flames, pouring across the floor and following the one who had called from the world above. Light of day did not prevent it from finding whom it sought. The smoke enshrouded the servant. As it lifted away, in place of the twisted shape stood a young man with black hair and pale skin. His eyes were the color of metal and until he learned the ways of humankind, they were devoid of any sense of emotion. He was thin and tall. His first steps stumbled, knocking him into a tree. He blinked, and he breathed.

Her smell was the first thing he remembered. In the gray world surrounding him, it was the only thing that meant anything. His longer legs were tricky to get used to, but once he learned to step, and step again, he found he could travel quite a distance without getting tired. Eventually, he did get tired, but that wasn't the first problem. Something inside him rumbled. He felt empty. Some trees he passed had round things dangling. Somewhere far back in his mind, in places he couldn't reach, memory made him want to bite into these things. What he took was hard, but he could eat. There was a subtle flavor. Different, but not bad. The rumbling eased. He took two more of the round things and continued.

Tiredness led to sleep. Sleep without dreams of the Dark Realm helped him feel stronger. Memory of the smell of innocence drove him to wake. Each day he sought the one but did not find her. His first sighting of people made him pause. Their limbs looked like his, but there were different sizes. Young ones were smaller. The old one bent. They spoke. He trailed them, listening.

Once more, something deep within him woke. Things started to make sense. There were names. Sky. Tree. Barn. Boy. Bath.

"Not sure where you're coming from, love, but you'll need to take a dip out by the barn. We're happy enough to welcome strangers to the table, but you have to be able to sit in the same room." An older woman with a large spoon pointed at a building across the property.

"Come on, lad." A man waved him on. "I'll show you what she means. Got you some fresh clothes to wear? What you got on could have come from the devil himself. Hopefully, they'll burn okay." He chuckled. "Got anything to say for yourself? What's your story?"

"I dunno." Part of the words came out as a whisper.

"Not much for talking, hey? Let's get you cleaned up and we'll see how you are."

There was a tub with water and stuff to rub on his skin. He couldn't quite smell, but he had a sense he was better off than he'd been. The clothes he'd worn were gone, but there were drawstring pants and a cambric shirt that opened at the neck. A vest helped keep the shirt in place.

"Maker have mercy, I'd not have recognized you except your all skin and bones." The old woman smiled at him. "What have you been eating?"

"Apples." He recognized the fruit.

"You're a man, love, and men need meat. Alright, have a seat at the table. We've another man shown up. Always room for strangers."

"You are a blessing," the other man declared, impressed with the plate of food set in front of him.

He wasn't sure what to think of it.

"What's your name, lad?"

The man was looking at him. He watched the others.

"I'm Stuie, one of the king's men. Storm cut me off, won't get back to the castle until tomorrow."

"I'm John." The man who'd led him to the barn used a utensil to stab a piece of meat on the plate.

He copied the movements.

"Well, boy?" Stuie grinned. "Aren't you going to tell us?"

He blinked. "I don't have one." Not that he could remember.

"Did you hit your head? Something wrong with you?" John leaned closer.

Stuie rubbed the whiskers covering his chin. "It's as though you been riven from the earth. How about we give you that as your name, until you can remember something else."

Riven? He wasn't sure why, but he felt the name suited him.

After breakfast, Stuie drew Riven aside. "Don't look like farming is for you. You may be slow, but you can carry a sword, I would think. Get you some meat and muscles on those bones and maybe you could put a soldier in training through the rounds. What do you think?"

There was little point wandering the countryside. He, Riven, didn't understand what the other man meant, but he could get him somewhere. The world was gray. The only thing that mattered was her. Everything else would help him survive until he could consume her. He nodded.

Four

They didn't leave that day. As evening darkened the world, Riven sat at a rough-hewn table across from an old woman. She didn't have teeth in her mouth the way most of the others did. She rested her wrists on the edges of a shallow bowl, picked up a long green plant and pulled it apart so the inside balls could fall into the bowl.

"Called shucking," she explained, showing him how to break the pod.

Riven mimicked her motions. She said other things, but he wasn't listening to her.

"Must have been hit hard," Stuie sharpened his sword with a stone as he chatted with another man.

"Not sure he's a safe one to take to Allington. Look of wild in his eyes."

Stuie shrugged. "Having no memory of self, world, or place in it could make any of us wild." Stuie paused a moment, catching Riven's eye. "No, he has something to be got."

"It's three day's journey. Can you do that without sleep?"

Stuie chuckled. "I've got half a horse in size on the

lad." In the next moment he frowned. "My own boy could be about his age. Perhaps providing for this unfortunate somehow could be aiding my son."

A son? Riven stared at the bowl. Life as the other thing he'd been wasn't fully remembered, but he knew well enough he hadn't been anyone's son.

~

Stuie moved them at a moderate pace along paths that later opened to roads. By the time they left the farm, their group had grown to include two soldiers and an archery master. Riven huddled within a cape that took on the color of the forest, though all he saw was gray. The old woman beckoned him to a chest. "Lift this for me. These old bones lack the strength they once had." She pushed aside something white then lifted what had been beneath. She presented Riven with the mound of woven fabric. "It's a cape," she explained as he held it. "Should keep you dry. A bit of warmth if the air turns chilly." At his blank stare, she showed him the clasp. He bent so she could place it across his shoulders.

He felt odd, as though for but a moment he was something other than gray. He turned without response.

As they traveled, the others kept their distance, except for Stuie. He put a sword in Riven's hands after they settled the first night. Riven studied it. Unlike the crudely forged weapon he'd used before, this one gleamed in the firelight. It moved with a whistle when he turned his hand. He could kill them all. Years within the Dark Realm taunted him. His hand tightened on the hilt, and he gave it another spin through the air. Memory of her scent stayed his hand. To find her, he needed others. He lowered the sword.

Stuie relaxed his grip on his own weapon. "Let's

try a few paces." He showed the first step to parry and thrust. He had him practice until the traveler stew bubbled over a small fire.

Three days continued much the same. When he wasn't practicing movements with the sword, Riven nestled within the cape focusing on the grim world surrounding him. When they arrived at the city, there wasn't time to observe the strange resemblance to what he knew of the Dark Realm. Stuie led them to the barracks, beyond which were training fields. A group of men coming from a path that led to the palace greeted them before they entered the building.

"Prince Snechtal," Stuie bowed, then kicked Riven to copy his movements.

"What is this?" Prince Snechtal peered at Riven. "Have you brought us a wild dog?"

"He's a bit untrained, but we need someone who can lead new soldiers through their paces. I think once he knows them himself, he'll do a good job."

Snechtal shrugged, unconvinced. "If you think so. Just make sure he's worth his keep."

By the end of the day, Riven had a bed in a room for himself, a change of clothes, a welt where Stuie wacked him with the flat of his sword, and food. There was no more rumbling inside himself. From the door of his room, he watched the black sky come alive with points of light. Dim dots of light, but they were there. Part of him wanted to hate them. But not all of him.

Five

For two years, Estellyn kept her word to her parents. She remained close to the farmhouse, helping her mother, watching her brothers leave for a season. One morning, Corman leaned back in his chair after breakfast and studied his only daughter. "Wandering the land around here won't prepare you to hike into the highlands with the herds. You show me you've built strength into your limbs, and you'll be ready next season."

Estellyn felt excitement stir. She glanced at mother. Molly nodded with a smile. As soon as the kitchen had been set to rights, Estellyn prepared a pack. Standing on the front porch of the farmhouse, she breathed the warming air. Birds sang, and specks of pollen glittered in beams of sunlight. Molly came up behind her, straightening the shoulders of Estellyn's pack. "Just a few days. Don't stay away too long."

Estellyn turned and hugged her mother. "I'll return before you've time to truly miss me."

Molly sighed. "You know how to take care of yourself better than the boys. Stay to the roads. Use the nicer sleep houses."

Estellyn kissed her cheek and grinned. "I'll start with this road right here," she said as she stepped off the porch, "and wander where I will." She let her feet lead her away from home.

The familiar trails led to roads. The Realm of Brennagh, often referred to as Overworld, though Estellyn didn't know why, had one major city, the capital house of the royal family. It was a two-day journey walking. Spring blooms decorated the landscape. After a few hours on a neat trail, she paused for a meal. Cool water rejuvenated her as much as the meat pie stuffed with mushrooms. She rinsed her fingers in a small stream of water. Wildflowers surrounded her. She picked a myriad of colors and wove herself a crown. A bee admired her work as she returned to the road.

When the sun dipped beyond the trees, Estellyn searched for a place to sleep. There were accommodations for a price. Mother's wish for her to use the better sleeping houses would mean an even higher price, but her preference was a place to watch the stars. Though light dwindled, she found a large tree with a burned-out wedge. The sleeping mat fit. She laid her head where she could watch points of light through the thick branches. Sounds of night lulled her to sleep.

As she lay dreamless, something stood close. It's single gleaming horn lit the leaves around it. With a shake of its head, it returned to the depths of the woods.

Chattering squirrels and a blue jay eager for a morsel woke Estellyn early. The faintest fog clung to the woods like a thin veil. She stretched. The cool air was invigorating, not biting. She followed the sound of water and found places to relieve herself and wash sleep from her face. Sitting on a rock watching the water flow, she combed through her hair which had grown nearly to her waist. She braided it then coiled the braid around her head so branches could not snare her. Though the flower crown wilted slightly, it nestled on her head. She packed her bag and returned to the road.

This day of journey led through more villages as she drew closer to the capital city of Allington. Rather than follow the road through the villages, Estellyn found her way around them. Trees in the orchards were blooming, too early for fresh fruit. She made do with what she brought from home. That night, there was no forest in which to seek shelter.

"You seem young to be traveling on your own." An older woman walked beside a dragging donkey.

Estellyn shrugged. "Father sent me to Allington to inquire of its markets." She was not comfortable with the lie.

She narrowed her eyes. "Should have arranged proper accommodation for you as well. My rooms are already let, but there's plenty of space in front of the hearth if you have your own sleeping mat. Hot meal, too."

"Are you sure?"

She smiled. "Borders keep me going since my mate died a few winters back. I don't think one more at the table will be a hinderance."

Estellyn followed her. The house was large, tucked between others of the same. It went up a couple of levels. The hearth was wide, and with a full belly and low fire, Estellyn slept soundly. A breakfast of eggs on toast tempted her from leaving at first light. The delay did not hurt, they were already quite close to the royal city.

What she was doing here, she wasn't certain. She

didn't have money for the markets. The city was built into a hillside. Standing near the gates, looking up, she tilted her head. The vantage from the top of the hill would give her a good view of everything. Rather than go through the main gates, she wandered some outlying areas. As she climbed, she observed fields and woods abutting the palace. There was movement in the fields. Drawing closer, she noticed most of the men were soldiers. Though their system of ranks was unfamiliar, men in red shirts gave direction to those who's uniforms were plain. The day warmed as the overhead sun beat down on the fields. Estellyn climbed a tree which offered shade as well as a view of the training. It seemed the young soldiers were being drilled on tactics and positions. The group she could see clearly worked with swords. Parry, thrust, turn—she could hear words being barked by the leaders. The men repeated the movements over and over. A large boy tripped more often than not. He'd swipe his forehead, push himself to his feet, and continue practice. Another slender boy offered a hand, but the bigger one shoved it aside. That, too, played out time and again.

When Estellyn could no longer bear sitting on a hard branch, she picked her way down. Fear of being seen made her move further into the trees surrounding the southeast edge of the castle. A large birch tree whose bark had peeled to reveal a smooth finish had a little alcove where she could eat. She retrieved a satchel with fruit and a wedge of bread and a skin of water. The ground was much more comfortable than the branch. She didn't mind sitting to eat. Sounds of the forest serenaded her. Whippoorwills called among the canopy of trees. Red birds chirped as they searched for insects crawling among the leaves. A family of rabbits hid in a burrow beneath a cracked rock. She could hear the scratches of the babies as they crawled through their dark homes. Ruckus from the field also added to the noise of the forest. Finished with her midday meal, she searched the tree. A little higher than her head, yet still within reach, was a broken nub of a branch. She hung her bag. "I guess I could leave this here." She talked to herself, rubbing her hands on her leggings. Not wanting to risk losing her things, she made a careful study of the area so she could find it once more, then crept closer to the fields to watch more.

For two days, she spent hours watching from the trees. On the second day, she changed her vantage point to a tree further west. Soldiers wore leather vests and leggings to protect themselves from hits of the weapons. The swords didn't look sharp. The slender young man spared with a different partner. He should widen his stance to make the other man work harder to strike. Not that she could give him actual pointers. He whirled his sword around and the other one lost his sword to the ground. What sort of trick managed that?

The warm muggy morning turned hot, and clouds thickened in the sky. Estellyn started the climb down, but the sleeve of her green tunic snagged on a branch and tore. She froze. Although it was a quiet noise, its strangeness might garner attention. The scrawny soldier stood closest to the trees. He twisted around, tilting his head as he looked. A bird hollered somewhere nearby, and the man shook his head while moving away.

Estellyn breathed as she rested her forehead against the tree. The tear could be mended, like the other roughly sewn spots. Though the green tunic fit better than when she started wearing it years ago, the color had faded, and it looked worn. She scrambled the rest of her way down. Her slightly larger boots made no sound when she landed on the ground. She headed away from the field.

Time had come to return home. From snatches of conversations she'd overheard, the woods led into the highland ridge. Though the path would not be as easy as the road, it should still require less time, a day perhaps. She needn't go into the highlands, just follow the ridge around until she came to familiar territory. Once she retrieved her bag and refreshed her supply of food for the journey home, she found the track. Going higher into the mountains meant the air cooled. She pulled her blanket and fastened it at her throat with a pin. It helped as she continued. She hadn't quite reached the ridge as day faded. An unused shepherd's hut stood among the trees. There was wood for a fire. Estellyn watched flames dance as she ate a small fruit pie after a wedge of beef and a carrot.

Something woke her in the night. The fire had died to embers. Light came through the small window. She frowned. It wasn't morning. Where did the light come from?

Nothing cautioned her to remain inside. She stepped through the door. Something white fluttered at the corner of her sight. She turned to look. An animal moved among the trees. When it stepped closer, Estellyn gasped. It was a horse, so white it gleamed. The horn in its forehead brought a memory. "I've seen you before. Are you the same horse? Is it possible?" Yet, she'd never seen another with a horn reaching toward the heavens.

It turned its head. Its eyes made Estellyn draw in a breath. They were starlight, and life, and every good thing she could bring to mind. It shook its head, as though acknowledging her awe and wonder. A moment later it moved to the trees. Estellyn wanted to follow. She ran back inside the hut, grabbed her things, shoving them into the bag. She didn't bother wrapping the blanket around her but hurried back outside. The horse was further away, but still easy to see. She went after it.

Estellyn couldn't explain why, but she knew the horse intended for her to follow. It led her from the path, but in places she could walk, and it stayed close enough to provide light so she wouldn't stumble. Morning came, and the horse moved further on. Estellyn never caught up with it, and yet, she never lost sight of it either. The air warmed, becoming thick with a threat of rain later in the day. She kept moving. Blowing tendrils of hair from her face, she climbed a hill. The forest opened. Her breath came hard and fast, but the horse thankfully stopped. With blue sky overhead, Estellyn flopped on her back on grass that was a mix of heather and clover. She breathed deeply; the feel of sunlight warmed her further. A stream guggled nearby. She sat up to look. It crossed the glen, at one point falling into a deep pool built with a ring of stones, then continued back into the forest. The horse drank from the pool. Its horn touched the water, causing sparkles to glimmer in the sunshine. After its fill of water, the horse munched on grass. Estellyn wiped sweat from her forehead. The water looked cool and refreshing. She moved to the pool, crouching to cup her hand and drink. The exertion of their climb faded away.

"I've never seen this place." She talked softly as she moved closer. The horse didn't seem to mind. She sat on a patch of grass and removed her boots. Once she pulled her leggings as high as they would go, she scooted to the edge of the pool. Smooth rocks lined the edge. It didn't have the natural qualities of the stream itself. "If someone made this, it was ages ago."

The horse didn't seem bothered by her voice or her presence. It moved closer to drink while she bathed her feet. Periodically, it ate grass.

"You must be the same horse. I remember your eyes. I'm glad you've kept yourself from trouble." Estellyn sighed as she dangled her feet in the cool water. She dipped her hands as well then rubbed her face. A moment of soaking refreshed her. She retrieved her boots and crossed to the other side of the stream. She sat in the sun to dry her feet. "It was cloudy below. Did you come up here to get out of rain? I know it was bound to start soon; the air was getting so thick."

A few minutes later, while she hooked a buckle, she noticed a white stick fallen over in some bushes. The stick looked as though someone had scraped off the bark and then sanded it smooth. She connected the final buckle on her boot and went to investigate.

It was a hard wood. Even when she hit it against a tree trunk hard enough to jar her hand, the stick didn't break. It was roughly the same width as her wrist. Held as a walking stick it came a little above her waist.

"I wonder if I could use this to practice moves like the soldiers?" She jabbed forward.

The horse sneezed and shook its mane, which rippled like silk, and then moved to the trees away from the pool. Estellyn held on to the stick as she jogged to catch up.

"I hope we're heading in the direction of the farm. I'd like to have dinner."

A little further on they passed into a thick batch of

shrubbery. "I need a path to walk. This is too thick to forge my own," she mumbled, but pressed on. The horse remained further ahead. Estellyn stumbled down an incline then found herself on a familiar path coming off the ridge. She'd run a few paces before she realized she no longer saw the horse. She was only a few hours from the farmhouse. She shifted her pack and used the walking stick.

~

Riven stacked fresh bales of hay for archery practice when a breeze brought her scent. His body went rigid. Nothing in the gray world around him changed. He turned. Soldiers had gone for their meal. The scent was fleeting, as though she had been there a moment and moved on.

He closed his eyes. She would be back. Now that he knew she could be close, he would watch with more diligence.

40

Six

"You've seen something," Molly noticed an unusual gleam in Estellyn's blue eyes.

"I went to the palace and watched soldiers train. Why have none of my brothers become soldiers?"

She laughed. "The work of herds takes many hands. Unless there is a threat of war, they are needed here."

"Morin is heading into the highlands soon. If I were to follow—I know father said to wait until next season, but the hard work of moving the beasts is done."

Molly shook her head. "Lewach is in the lower field. Help him."

"Or I can go with Morin and Estellyn take care here," Lewach said as he leaned over Molly's shoulder. "I'll have a few days to teach what she doesn't already know. Father is here if there is a need."

Estellyn stood. "A good start for what I will learn next season."

"If your father will agree to it," Molly frowned at Lewach.

He grinned. "Already done."

~

Long deep lowing whirled across gently rolling hills. Estellyn climbed on the rock wall marking the outer fields of the midland farm. Amber-colored cows contrasted with the deep green grass. The animals strolled, their wide hoofs able to manage the dips and gullies where the hills punched into each other. Two young cows, horns barely sticking out of the side of their head, bounded after a larger one. The adult shook its head, causing the long hair over its eyes to temporarily flow back. It huffed, and the little ones scurried away. Estellyn sighed. She promised to watch the herd now that Lewach went into the highlands with the others, but there was little of interest to do for the passing of time.

A circle of trees provided shelter from potential weather. A long ago relative burned out one of the trees to form a cupboard for supplies. Estellyn grabbed an apple from a basket on a shelf. She took a bite, then studied her staff as she chewed. Not a real sword, but perhaps she could use it to practice? She took three more bites from the apple before tossing the rest of it across the way. She used a portion of water to clean her fingers before lifting the staff with her right hand. As with the first moment she touched the smooth stick, her fingers tingled. She tilted her head to study it closer. Its color was a blend of cream and soft yellow. There were no carvings or shapes forged in it, yet it was straight though slightly tapered toward one end. She turned it around in her hand, brandishing it in the air, and she almost imagined a sword. What had she seen, watching the soldiers?

She closed her eyes and concentrated on the days she'd spied on the castle and the grounds where soldiers practiced. One man swung his sword back and forth.

Estellyn stood. The staff didn't have a handle, or whatever they called the end where it was held. She wrapped her hand about a foot-span from the end. Making an eight, she swung back and forth. The other end felt heavier, so she switched sides. This time, the staff seemed to balance, and it traveled smoothly first one way than the other. She switched hands. Though the motions did not feel as natural as her right hand, the left still managed to swoop back and forth in an eight-shape.

She brought the staff where she could see the cows. With no one around, it seemed harmless to practice some of the moves she'd witnessed. The cows remained beyond reach. Estellyn stood straight with the staff pointed upward, then she jabbed forward as she moved her right leg. She tried it again while moving forward with her left leg. The stance was firmer, but the reach of a sword would be lessened. She switched back, and repeated the move over and over, adding a shout as she lunged.

The little cows moved closer to investigate, others paid absolutely no attention.

~

Even when her turn to watch the cows ended for the season, Estellyn continued to use the unsettled parts of the farm and woods. The tone of her arms tightened as she practiced a variety of moves. Trees received wallops. A large cow remained unfeigned even as it was threatened. The overhead sun heated the afternoon. Estellyn allowed her tunic to fall around her waist. Her undershirt grew damp with sweat. She grabbed a skin of water and drank. She was wiping a drip of water from her lip when she heard a sneeze.

Her body stilled and tightened. She reached for her

staff leaning against the tree where she'd hung two skins of water. She slipped around the trunk to move from the line of sight. There was another sneeze. Estellyn shook her head, then called out in a deep low voice. "You might as well show yourself. The mountain and half the forest have heard you."

A young man in soldier uniform moved forward, coming out from a grove of trees. His hair was darker than hers and from the shadow of hair growing across his face, he was slightly older as well. He cleared his throat. "I was surprised to see you practicing here. I didn't expect to find anyone on my walk."

Estellyn shrugged on her tunic then tugged it into place. "No one travels these lands."

"Then what are you doing here?"

"I work for the farmer. These are his lands."

The young man chuckled. "Wouldn't it be truer to say these are the king's lands? Farmers don't own property."

"Are you a king's man? He receives his tribute, or so I believe. He wouldn't do as well tending it himself."

"That's true. Doubt he's capable of it on his own."

"His talents lie elsewhere." Estellyn tapped her staff on the ground.

The stranger pointed at it. "You use it like a sword? Have you had training?"

She shrugged. "Only what I've seen." She pointed at the sword he strapped to his side. "Have you had practice?"

"I am far too thirsty to battle it out today. I neglected to bring water with me."

She only paused a moment before making an offer. "I have an extra skin. Walk me through some of the sword exercises you do as a soldier, and I'll give you the water."

"There's a reason why ladies don't get to be soldiers."

"I don't want to be a soldier I want to be able to defend myself. A sword doesn't care who's blood it spills."

"That has to be in the one wielding it." He moved closer. "I see your point. Okay, give me water to drink and I will work you through the first two basic moves."

She tossed him a half full skin.

He drank, wiped moisture from his lips, and then waved at her walking stick. "Do you have a sword? What you're holding won't last against real metal."

Estellyn lifted it. "Doesn't seem to get a mark when I hit the trees."

"A tree is not the same as the turned metal used to forge this weapon." He pulled out his sword.

Estellyn held the staff, lengthwise, in both her hands. She spread her feet slightly apart. "Strike it and let's see what happens."

He moved closer, then made certain the sword wasn't near enough to her to risk an injury. "Don't move your hands." He warned as he raised and lowered the sword to the staff. He struck with a light force. Estellyn felt the energy of it in her arms, but she managed to keep hold of the staff.

He frowned, rubbed his hand along the wood, then looked at her. "Let me try this one more time. It should at least have made a mark on the wood."

He tried again, with the same result. Estellyn was smiling. "Can we try the basic moves now?"

"Alright." He pointed at her staff. "I want to know

what kind of wood that is made from."

"I found it… somewhere else. Now tell me how I should stand for this first move."

He sighed, but stood beside her, pointing at her feet to mimic him. He led her through a set of swings.

"What's your name?" the stranger asked as he countered her swing with a grunt.

She copied the movement of his feet. "Have you earned a name? Why do you wander the highlands alone?"

"I heard rumor of an ancient beast seen within the wilds."

"A dragon? The cows would be in danger."

"No dragons. We haven't had their like since my great grandfather's age. No, this is a beast of purity. A unicorn."

She changed her tactic, swinging the staff in a reverse movement, but the stranger parried the move. "What is a unicorn? I've never heard any stories."

"Haven't you? It looks like a horse with a long horn growing from its forehead."

Estellyn stopped. "A white horse?"

"Yes, white, with a beautiful mane and tail."

"What would be the significance of such an animal?"

"Have you seen a unicorn?"

"What would be its significance?"

He stood silently for a moment, gazing as though to weigh her merit. At length, he explained. "The Maker sent creatures of light and goodness to wander our world. Those who see one will be imbued with courage and strength if they are good. Others will cower with fear. During times when evil forces seek to war with our world, the unicorn will choose champions, those who are pure of heart and capable to stand against evil."

"Champion? The kingdom is at peace. Nothing evil stirs." Even as she spoke, a cold breeze made a shiver crawl down her back.

"All is not as it should be. An old seer in the village of Hoth swore to my brother he would be dead by winter if he allows the dark one's servant to remain in his employ."

"Why would he have a servant of the dark lord?"

"He doesn't, at least not to his knowledge. Then someone said a unicorn had been seen along the Highland ridges. I thought if I come, if I were chosen, I could save my brother's life."

"What I saw is a horse. We have several working in the fields."

"What of the horn?"

"An abnormality."

"Tell me what you saw."

But Estellyn didn't want to share. "There's nothing to tell. I have to leave."

"Wait, please! You haven't even told me your name."

"I say the same to you."

"Jeremian. My name is Jeremian."

She laughed. "As in prince?"

"I have too many older brothers for that to make a difference."

She bowed. "Prince Jeremian. Thank you for the lesson. I hope you find what you seek." She left her belongings and ran carrying only the staff and was soon gone from sight.

"Wait, please…"

She heard his cry. There was something truthful about him. *No, he is a liar.* Her mutterings didn't alleviate the heavy feeling in her gut.

As she found a trail leading to the ridges, she slowed. *What if I find the pool? I can prove the white horse is nothing more. If it is there.*

Seven

A few hours of walking brought her to the thicket on a steep slope of mountain. The walking stick helped her forge a way through. She hissed as a long thorn cut into the back of her hand. She wiped the blood on her tunic and kept going. She would have missed the right way, but the sound of running water perked her ears. She turned, climbed, and fell into the glen. She rolled onto her back and just lay and breathed for a time. Until a horse neighed.

She rolled over and looked. The horse with its white horn watched her from the other side of the stream. "You are a unicorn, aren't you?"

As he'd said. Estellyn sat up and crossed her arms. The animal gazed with its shimmering eyes, a steady intelligent glance that made her lower her head contrite.

"Do not chide the young woman for her lack of knowledge." A tall slender woman stepped into the clearing. Light emanated from her, causing glints to run across the heathered grass beneath her feet. Estellyn gasped, wanting to run, and yet held in place. The woman looked at Estellyn with silver eyes aglow in starlight. "You have naught to fear of me."

"What are you?"

She tucked her hair behind a pointed ear. "Do you not recognize an Elf when you see one?"

"Elves aren't real," Estellyn shook her head.

"Are we not? What a funny thing to say." She walked to the horse—unicorn, Estellyn forced herself to use its name, and rubbed a hand along its flank. "You sought *her* today. This is a first."

"I sought who?"

"Astebery, the Unicorn. Morgeth captured her, intending to sacrifice her at the feast of the dead. She drew you to save her."

Estellyn didn't want to hear. "All I did was find a horse bound in a cave. I freed her." She glanced at the unicorn. "It. As I would have any free-spirited animal."

"Yet you know better."

"What about Jeremian? He wants to be her champion."

"The princeling? How have you met him?"

"He barged into my haven, claiming to seek the unicorn."

"Hm." She pulled a cup from a bag that hung on a tree. She walked to a cut in the hill where water washed down from the heights and filled the cup.

Estellyn thought about her water skins hanging where she'd left them in the woods closer to home. Instead of focusing on her own thirst, she tried asking questions of the stranger. "Who are you?"

"My name is Lystra. You are Estellyn Rose."

"You know my name?"

"Riding a unicorn reveals many thoughts and things of a person. You kept nothing from her. That is how she knew."

Estellyn crossed her arms. "Knew what?"

Lystra sat on a carpet of grass. "That can wait. Join me?"

Chewing her lip didn't make the choice easier. Strangeness surrounded the Elf woman. Estellyn felt the hairs on her arms shiver… she didn't want to know why.

Lystra offered a kind smile. "What do you know of unicorns?"

"Jeremian said the Maker sent them to be light in our world."

"You believe in the Maker?"

"We come from somewhere." She looked down, toying with her hair. "That cave, something there is evil. I could feel it. Horse," she rolled her eyes at the rebuking grunt from the animal. "I mean unicorn. She is completely not what… whatever is down there."

"Your sense does you credit. The Dark Realm has a dark lord, Morgeth, although he is paler than moonlight. His thoughts and his deeds are dark. He wants to destroy Astebery and her kind." Lystra peered at Estellyn. "He wants to consume you."

A shiver crawled across her skin. "Me? Why? How could he know of me?" She crossed the stream and sat close to Lystra. "What… what do you mean consume?"

"Most people will never see a unicorn. They don't have the spirit to see."

"There's nothing special about me."

She laughed. "There's something very special about you. Astebery chose you."

"I was the only one nearby. What choice did she have?"

Again, Lystra laughed. "A unicorn has the gift of creation. They can heal and build, bring light and joy-when they are in the hands of good. Evil can use them for destruction."

"You said he was going to kill her."

Lystra glanced at Astebery again. "Not if I can help her." Astebery shook her mane with a snort. "True, what real purpose brought you today?"

Estellyn rolled the staff in her lap. Blue sky shone overhead. Water babbled over rocks as it scurried across the glen. Breezes blew, causing leaves on the trees to sway to unheard music. She stared at the bush where the staff had laid. "I don't know much about swords or weapons of any kind, but Jeremian's sword couldn't break this." She tapped the staff on the ground.

"Why do you think that is?"

"She led me here and gave it to me."

"A gift?"

"What is it? Why me?"

Lystra glanced at the unicorn then back to Estellyn. "I don't know. You will have to learn that yourself."

"Is there time? Jeremian seemed to think the unicorn is a herald to war with the Dark Realm."

Lystra nodded. "War will come, but not yet. Building his armies takes time."

"What of our armies? Should they know there is danger?"

"It will take more than the force of men to defeat Morgeth. You must train; prepare yourself."

Estellyn meant to protest further, but Astebery stepped close enough to nuzzle her shoulder. Joy of her simple touch removed doubts and concerns.

Lystra stood. "Wash your hand in the stream. It will heal your wound. Drink, and your thirst will quench."

Estellyn did as she was bade. "Then what?" She

turned, but the glen was empty. She stood alone. It was late afternoon and would be a warm summer night. Rather than travel in the dark, she chose to remain. The blue sky faded, and stars shone in the sky. The heather in a culvert formed by tree roots proved comfortable enough for sleep. She tucked her arm beneath her head and stared at the twinkling lights far above. Sometime in the night, she woke to the moon staring at itself in the pool. Its light bounced around her. She stood, and not sure why, she danced in circles, her bare feet light on the grass. As she twirled, it seemed as though others joined her: tall, splendid figures dancing in delight of moonlight. In the reflection of the pool, she thought she saw a woman smiling, one who looked like herself, yet not her. The image was startling real, causing Estellyn to falter in her dance and stare. A cloud covered the moon, dissipating the light.

Estellyn awoke with a start. Morning had come. She blinked. An odd dream for an odd place. She reached for her boots, then paused. Dirt and bits of clover stuck to her feet. She swallowed. More than a dream? Rather than consider the possibility, she moved to the stream and washed away the dirt. It didn't take long for the warm morning to dry her skin. She donned her boots. Time to go home.

54

Eight

As Estellyn made her way to the farmhouse, a gray bird swirled through the air above and landed on a flat deck beside a chimney. She jogged the rest of the way home, rushing in breathless. "They sent a bird, is everyone alright?"

Corman stood. "A bird? Are you sure?"

"I saw it land on the roof."

"I will check." He returned a short while later with a note in his hand. "Calves have been birthed on the trail." He shook his head. "They should have noticed the heifers hadn't dropped yet. We'll likely lose them."

"If they haven't gone too far, I could bring them down."

"He says they passed the shelter at Osbeng." He considered the note and her for a while.

Estellyn waited. She hadn't been that high into the upper fields, but it should still be the easier route.

"You could take a wagon. Get Callum or Lachlan to stay and help load them. The calves follow their mothers. Bring them to the field here with the other spring births."

Estellyn dug her nails into her hands to keep from

grinning widely. "I may go?"

He nodded. "You're smart with weather. If it looks like a storm, stay in the shelter until it passes."

"Understood. I'll get ready."

"I'll have the wagon with the stock pull set in place at the front of the house."

She'd had a little practice with stock used to pull wagons and other machinery on the farm. This one was a large gray beast with a hump between its shoulders and a low head. Once Corman and the farm were out of sight, Estellyn dropped the reins on the bench beside her. "You know where to go, you don't need me pulling on you." The beast used slow steady steps. "I should call you something," she spoke to it as though it could understand her. "Boghlas, because you are a gray thing." It turned onto a narrow lane. She leaned forward at the initial incline, but it leveled, and the ride became smooth. To one side were trees and woods, on the other tall grasses swayed in a breeze she could not yet feel. The sun had passed overhead when she saw a shelter surrounded by a low fence. Beyond, the rugged highlands swept upward.

Lachlan waved. "Father did send you."

She shrugged. "He has two dozen calves to watch over. Safer to send me."

"You'll do fine, though it's too late to load them tonight."

Estellyn jumped to the ground. "Show me where the bridge boards are before you head up."

"I'll stay until morning. Get you on your way."

"I've helped load heifers before. They need you with the rest of the herds."

Lachlan considered, then nodded. "Over this way." He led her into the shelter. "Show me you can line up your wagon, and I'll leave you to it."

Estellyn went to Boghlas. "We have this." Together, they parked the wagon where the boards could be locked in place.

"Well done. I'll leave you the campfire. Already has stew. Haven't seen signs of predators but stay alert." With that, he grabbed his pack and left, disappearing behind the shelter.

The day waned. Stars blazed across the backdrop of night. Clear mountain air revealed more than could be seen on the farm or in the village. One of the calves mooed long and quiet. Its mother muzzled the furry beast, tucking it close by her side. The other two already slept with their mothers. Estellyn let the fire die down. Even in the dark she could see the wood structure that looked like a small barn. One side built against the mountain and the other opened to the vista of fields and highlands. The structure had a roof, helpful if rain set in.

A different light drew closer. At first, Estellyn hid in the shelter, but what came was the unicorn. Two of them. Astebery and another, a stallion. They seemed agitated, prancing across the field. Estellyn walked from the shelter. One of the mother cows glanced at the pair of unicorns coming closer and gave an unusual call. The three grown cows stood while their calves slumbered. Astebery shook her mane which gleamed with starlight. The cows dropped their heads as though acknowledging royalty. Estellyn glanced from the unicorns to the cows. What had Lystra said about the unicorns being sent by the Maker?

Something dark moved in the field. Her attention fell from the cows' odd greeting of the unicorns. Her body stiffened. She set her feet at a comfortable distance and stood holding her staff. What moved nearer tried to conceal itself among brush and trees at the edge of the highlands, but Estellyn managed to track its movement. She stepped further away from the shelter and the animals. When the thing was within distance to strike with a rock from her pocket, she called out. "Strangers have no place here. Be gone. Depart unharmed."

"Stranger? I have walked these lands for many lifetimes." The voice of the creature was low and slow, language not part of its traditions. "I have not traveled for you."

"Your journey is a vain one tonight." Estellyn tightened her grip on the staff. "Go back."

An odd thing happened. Light brightened. The creature stood like a man, but his arms were longer. The contours of his face gave him a twisted scowl with bulging eyes. Three rings pierced the bridge of its nose. Its hand lifted to block light. "Why do you come against me with your tricks?" It snarled. "Those dumb creatures escaped my Master. I am sent to retrieve them."

"I am not unaware of their significance. Be gone, goblin."

It tried stepping closer, but the light increased. With a painful scowl, it staggered back. "Someday you will stand in the presence of my Master, and you will feel the sting of his hand."

"I am nothing to your master."

"You have made yourself known unto him. He will have you." With that, the creature turned and scurried away. Light diminished until the stars gleamed overhead once more. Her skin tingled with energy. She turned around. The unicorns ate grass. The cows returned to their babies. Boghlas watched her. The world had righted, but she stood trembling for a long while before dozing beside the animals.

She jerked awake. A slight chill touched the highlands. As she pulled a blanket from the wagon, she realized the unicorns had gone. There was no sign the fiend had come back for them. A faint circle of light still glowed at the perimeter. She pulled the blanket around her and stared at overhead stars. Something in her shook, whether from what she'd seen or the power flowing through the staff, she did not know. It lay on the ground within arm's reach. It still looked like a branch smoothed and oiled. Mostly smoothed. She frowned, noticing ridges in a thin line. She rolled it slightly toward her. Those weren't ridges. They were words, a stream of words in a single line running from top to bottom. They hadn't been there before. At least, she hadn't noticed them before. The language looked nothing like the bits of script she'd memorized. But reading language wasn't encouraged, except with royalty and their charges.

Jeremian came to mind. Estellyn rubbed her finger over the words. Curiosity of the mysterious message on the staff outweighed her distrust of the young royal who disrupted her lesson. Throughout the morning, she wracked her brain for other options as they returned to the farmlands, but there was no one else. She led the calves and their mothers to the barn near the main farmhouse. She filled a travel satchel, glancing through a window to check sky patterns.

Nine

Beneath the great throne room within the Dark Realm, a series of pillars and arches supported a vast undercroft. Morgeth paced the cold depth, expecting an arrival. The breeding pools were close. The sacrifice could easily be dragged to the sandy shores. His ears twitched at the sound of footsteps. As his steps slowed, his temper rose. He recognized the essence of the one he'd sent to capture the unicorn. But the unicorn was not with him.

He turned. "Did you leave my prize in Overworld?"

The goblin, Dreit, snarled. "Not by choice. They were protected. A power not one I can break."

"The unicorn holds the power of creation, but it cannot protect itself against you." The words the slave spoke suddenly registered, and Morgeth turned. "They? Someone was with the unicorn?"

"It was a pair of the beasts. A mare and a stallion. And a girl protecting them."

"A girl?" Morgeth hissed. "A seasoned warrior should not be able to stand against you. What do you mean, a girl?"

The goblin snarled, showing jagged teeth. "She wielded something I could not pass."

Morgeth grabbed the beast, digging his nails into its head. Its howl could not free it from Morgeth's grasp. "Show me." Morgeth's cheeks darkened as he dug into the memory foils of the goblin. There were two unicorns. The chase started with the mare, but a stallion roared against him, slowing the goblin. The two were faster. Dreit tracked them into the midlands, then across the lower jut of the mountain lands. A field bathed in night revealed the creatures, and then the girl. Strange though she was, the wand in her hand drew attention. The image faded. Morgeth grasped Dreit by the throat and dug further, but life drained away too quickly, and he could draw no more from the corpse. He released his hold. Blood dripped from his hand. Rather than waste the substance, he made the trek to the pools.

A pair of unicorns? How long till they provided offspring? The waters of the pools lapped gently along sandy shores. An army had barely begun to propagate. The process needed to quicken.

Morgeth cursed Dreit's failure to obtain the unicorns as he returned to the throne room. The girl who stood with the unicorn reminded him of the one sought by another of his servants in Overworld. He crossed the hall to the massive fireplace where black fire burned continuously. He reached for shadows of smoke billowing from its depths. "Bring him to me."

~

Riven turned on the narrow cot. Something caused him to wake. He watched darkness pour through the window opening into his room. For a moment, he thought dreams had returned, but he sat up. Night held no fear for him. The darkness did not dismay. It curled around his feet. He tilted his head and watched it crawl along his legs then his torso. As it enveloped him fully, he gave himself to its purpose.

~

The thin pale man that soon appeared held no semblance to the goblin it had once been. Morgeth narrowed his eyes. "You are different."

Riven's eyes rested on the black fire. "I have learned what I need to be among them. I wait for her to return."

"She has been at the palace?"

He nodded. "I caught her scent. Not enough to follow, so I wait."

"They have given you a name." Morgeth sensed. His hold was strong. Nothing of the boy that had been twisted into goblin remained.

"Riven."

It suited, though the man would likely never know why. "Another servant encountered her. Go to the place I send you and trace her steps."

Riven's eyes gleamed with hunger not satisfied by food. "I will have her?"

Morgeth narrowed his eyes. "She must come to me first."

Riven's hands clenched. He wanted to refuse, yet Morgeth knew he would not.

~

Estellyn slid to the side of the window and watched. Something moved in the line of trees, more than a shadow. A few moments later, she saw a man. He was tall with dark hair and dark clothes. Not the night visitor with its twisted form, this was a young man, uncertain. He watched the house, moving to and from the cover of the trees.

Estellyn did not want to meet him. She crossed the house to the back kitchens where doors opened into the gardens. Paths starting on the far side of the gardens led to a narrow river. She pulled the satchel onto her back then covered up with a light cape with a hood that could be pulled over her head to block most of her face from sight. She didn't need the hood yet. Walking softly through rain-moistened paths, she made her way to the river.

A thick line of rope connected the dock of river boats with the other side of the river. She could take a boat and use the line to cross, or she could release the line and paddle further downstream. She glanced back. Whoever watched the farm hadn't made it around to the back yet. Estellyn placed her walking stick in the bed of a boat, unhooked the ferry line, then hoisted herself onto a middle seat. She used a paddle to push away from the short dock. With the boat in the middle of the river, the current swept it south. It was a different way to get to Allington, faster than walking. She checked the stick as the boat glided through water. The line of writing remained. Hopefully, Jeremian was done searching for the unicorn and he would be at the palace where she could find him.

~

They were not her, but her scent permeated everything. He wanted to tear something from them and wrap himself in it. Something he did not understand kept him from ripping life from them. As darkness surrounded the house and they settled for the night, he walked through the rooms silent as a ghost. Her space was obvious. He fell on his knees and let her essence wash through him. He took the blanket from her bed, then wanted to explore further. In a back cupboard, in a small box, lay a silver necklace. The pendant hurt his eyes, flashing something that came from beyond the gray world he knew. He left it laying across the shelf, unable to bear its touch to return it to its box. His chest ached and his hands shook. He gripped the blanket and hurried from the house. Travelling through the night, he could be back in his barrack by morning.

Ten

"Jeremian," Estellyn called from a stand of trees, just loud enough to grab his attention and none of the others.

He turned, moved slowly until he recognized her. He glanced at the other soldiers, but none paid attention to him. He jogged toward the trees. "What are you doing here?"

"I need your help. Something's happened."

A whistle blew across the field and an older man hollered. Jeremian glanced at the field then back to Estellyn. "I need to go. I'll bring my meal after we finish this exercise."

Estellyn nodded. "I'll be here."

~

Riven gasped at the smell on the air. It was her. His blood tingled at the memory of her. With a careful watch he turned. Prince Jeremian worked with a marksman quilling arrows. Riven shivered. The scent was on Jeremian. The young prince had met the cursed woman. From the stench on him, he'd spent time in her company.

"Don't much like him, I wonder."

"The boy hasn't a wicked bone in his body. Don't

see why you should loath him."

Two soldiers, one a thick red man with a long scar on his cheek and the other a man with a pocked face that resembled oatmeal, talked at him.

"What do you want?" Riven hunched over, lowering his head so he only had to look at their boots.

"The way you're watching him, some might wonder… but there's no denying hatred in your glance."

"He took something I wanted."

"That is indeed a problem." The ruddy soldier rubbed his beard.

The other nodded. "Should you do something about it?"

"I have no position." He peeked at them then lowered his head once more. "Unlike you. Your positions are… useful."

The ruddy soldier pulled a pipe from his jacket. "Unfortunate accidents have been known to happen in a weapon's field."

The sallow-skinned man nodded. "Last week, Averon took a blade with his foot."

"It would be a shame for the prince to suffer an accident."

"A permanent accident?" River clenched his fists.

"At least not one he's likely to come out of."

The pocked soldier crossed his arms. "What would you do for us to arrange such an accident?"

Riven tapped down his desire to show them exactly what would happen if they didn't do this thing. "I have access to rooms of vast wealth. If you were to know a time when a room were to be left unlocked and unguarded, you would have a few moments to choose among the least of the treasures."

~

Estellyn didn't need to hear more. The tall thin man dressed in black made her uneasy. Was he the same man she'd seen at the farmhouse? Careful movement through the tree meant she landed on the ground without alerting anyone to her presence. She retrieved her staff and backtracked to a trail that would take her around the southern yard of the castle.

Jeremian crossed blades with a thick man a few inches taller. He kept both hands on his sword, yet he still appeared to shake when the man struck him. Jeremian danced, more agile on his feet than his opponent. With a triumphant grin, Jeremian launched from a rock and swatted the other man with the flat of his blade. He quickly backed away.

With a grunt, the bigger man went off to search for someone else. Estellyn picked up a rock and threw it into Jeremian's shoulder. He spun with a curse, battle-ready. He frowned, checked the area around him, then smiled when he saw her. He jogged to meet her. Estellyn backed away.

"Wait," he called.

She rolled her eyes. "In here. No one needs to see your business."

He met her in the trees. "What are you doing here? I told you to wait at the other place."

But Estellyn saw the other soldiers on the trail from the upper field. "We have to go, now."

"Go where?"

"They want to kill you. One of your servants ordered it."

"I've already explained…"

"I don't know why; I only know what I heard. They

plan for you to have an accident in the field. Preferably one you won't recover from."

Jeremian let her lead him further away, but then stopped. "I need to get things. I can't run into the wild without supplies."

"It's too dangerous."

He pointed further south. "There's an entrance to the castle. Its underground. They won't see me."

She shook her head, but he already sprinted away. She chewed her lip. Someone needed to watch, to make sure the plotters weren't in his way. The two soldiers glanced around, then headed back toward the upper field. Estellyn kept to the trees but went in the same general direction. The other man was close. So close, she could reach out and touch him. Not certain why she did, she placed her hand on his arm. Cold seeped through her fingers. His eyes alighted on her and deepened with hatred and something more. The force of his stare caused her heart to pound in her chest. Neither of them seemed capable of moving for a moment.

Strange, the skin beneath her fingers didn't stay cold. A moment later, the man fell to the ground.

Jeremian stood behind him with his fist wrapped around the butt of his sword. "Come on, let's go." He pulled her along with him into the trees.

She allowed it, her mind still reeling from the encounter. "Who was he?"

"I think they call him Riven. What were you doing? He could have harmed you."

"I knew he was the one engaged to kill you. I meant to impede his progress. But when I touched him..." She shivered.

Jeremian halted in shadow of a large tree. "What?"

"He felt dark and cold. Not the way a man should feel."

~

Riven clawed his way back to consciousness. His head hurt. Something burned. He moaned as he pushed himself to his hands and knees. She had been there. She had touched him. His arm radiated with memory of her fingers. He turned and sat on the ground.

Light shone on him, something he'd never experienced before. He whimpered. The gray world, what happened to it? He rubbed his eyes, ran his hands across his head to the tender spot where he'd been hit. He pressed against it and reeled with pain. White splotches danced in his eyes. He hung his head between his knees until the waves of pain faded. His mind blanked and he squeezed his eyes. The Dark Realm, his hideous self, Master the only source of light in the dark—his memories were there. He forced the trembling to stop. He'd open his eyes and see the world as it should be—a gray-washed bitter space. He opened his eyes.

Light brought tears.

LAURIE LEE

Eleven

"Wait," Estellyn said as she pulled against Jeremian, regaining her sensibilities. "My stuff."

"There's no time."

"I have to get it. To show you. It's the reason I returned today." She changed course. Jeremian followed. She led him to the carved-out tree. They were close enough to the castle to hear scrimmages on the field and yet not be seen. She shoved a satchel at him. He slung it across his shoulder. She grabbed the staff, and they ran.

He wanted to move toward the river, but she pulled him along a different trail leading toward the highland ridges. "It's the only place I know we can be safe."

He motioned for her to lead. After a while of walking in silence, she glanced at him. "What made you hit him? How did you know?"

"I've noticed him watching for a while, since I first met you. When I saw the two of you," he shook his head. "I've never seen fear in you. I struck him."

Hours passed. Jeremian found apples ripe enough to eat.

Estellyn shared her oat cake. "It's not much, but it satisfies hunger and gives energy to keep moving."

"As long as I have water to wash it down." He held

up his full water sack.

Late morning on the second day of hiking, they stopped in a circle of trees near a main road.

"You think someone will follow us?" Estellyn asked as she watched the empty road.

Jeremian shrugged. "An uneasy feeling. I don't know if it means a threat is near or just knowing someone wants me dead. There's no reason to kill me."

"We've just a little further now." She adjusted the pack on her back. "You may meet someone where we go."

"Who?"

She shook her head. "Wait and see. I can tell you no more." Once again, she took the lead. The road remained empty the few miles they walked. There was no path where she drew him away. They pushed through undergrowth, using thin trees to pull themselves along the steep hill. Both breathed heavily as they reached an area where trees thinned. Estellyn grabbed Jeremian's sleeve to halt him. Through the trees, they spied the white unicorn prancing at the far end of the clearing.

Jeremian gasped. He walked two steps beyond the trees then fell to his knees, head bowed. The unicorn reared, hoofed legs dancing in air. Earth shook when she landed. Estellyn felt her strength. The animal crossed the clearing, splashing water as she kicked her feet up. She looked at Estellyn, still standing among the trees, and at the man kneeling before her. Her head tilted as she drew closer. Estellyn held her breath. The horn of the unicorn gleamed golden in sunlight except for a line of silver that coiled from tip to base. She touched Jeremian, brushing his hair with the horn. Once finished, she backed up and shook her head, the white mane moving around her like a blaze of glory. Then she pranced away, dancing across the clearing to where she'd been.

Estellyn felt her heart start beating again. "What are you doing?"

Jeremian remained kneeling but looked up. "The unicorn is a sacred animal, a blessed animal." He glanced at her, his face glowing with joy. "She touched me. Surely that means I am accepted as her champion?"

Estellyn giggled as she ran fingers through his lanky hair. "She did more than touch you." A lock of brown now gleamed silver.

They sat side by side, silently watching the unicorn eat. The day was warm. Sun gleamed overhead. Estellyn lay back with her arms behind her head, closing her eyes. Her hand tingled from touching the other man. Riven. She pushed thoughts of him away. It seemed unnatural to bring him to mind in this place.

"She's gone," Jeremian said, sadness tinged his voice.

Estellyn sat up. "We should stay. This is a safe place to spend the night."

Jeremian jumped to his feet. "Are you ready to practice more moves with a sword?"

She grabbed her walking stick with a smile. "Always."

They practiced throughout the afternoon. He showed her the trick to disarm someone, but she didn't have it yet.

"Enough, mercy," he finally laughed. "How about a fire and making sure we have more than apples for a meal this evening?"

"Shouldn't be hard to catch some rabbits, as long as you're willing to skin them."

He grinned. "If you want to fight with a sword, you need to get used to some blood and guts."

Before night settled over them, meat crackled on a fire. Jeremian took care of the skin and Estellyn turned a spit.

Jeremian checked on potatoes. "You said you came to the castle for a reason but never told me why."

"There are words written on the staff, but I don't read. You're a royal. You've probably been taught to read languages."

He frowned. "The staff you fought with? There's nothing on it."

"There wasn't, but there is now."

"Why? What would cause—"

"I was bringing calves down from the fields. Two unicorns came upon us. Astebery and a male. Something stalked them. Something evil."

Jeremian sat straight. "You saw two unicorns? Are you certain?"

She glared. "I never learned to read. I know how to count. Light came from the staff. It scared the hunter away."

"Unicorns live in solidarity except when they mean to mate. A foal is rare. Hundreds of years may pass before another one is birthed."

"I don't know anything about that."

"But if a unicorn gives birth a dragon will come forth as well."

Estellyn scoffed. "Don't be ridiculous. There are no dragons."

He shook his head. "Dragon eggs rest undisturbed within the earth for hundreds, maybe thousands of years. A baby dragon needs nothing of parents to survive."

"Why would it matter?"

"My grandfather spoke of a battle long ago. Ages ago, even. There was a dark lord and the dragon he used destroyed many lands. The unicorn's champion defeated the dragon, but it still took all the lands to drive the dark lord back into his lair. Rather than remain as separate countries, the Realm of Brenagh was formed."

"I've heard stories of Brenagh, but never about a dragon." She poked at the meat. "This is ready."

They ate, and what little conversation they had turned to comparing life in a palace with that of a farmhouse.

Estellyn settled for sleep with the fire between them. Thoughts of dragons played into her dreams. She woke before the morning. Night surrounded their camp. The fire had died down. Overhead, stars shimmered. She rolled onto her back and named them.

"Our people call that Renowyth, the dancers."

Lystra sitting beside her in the night wasn't as startling as it should be.

"Why do your people have different names for things?"

"Don't you mean our people?"

Estellyn sat up. "I know my father. He is not an elf."

"There was a terrible storm when you were born. Your mother lost her way. The farmers took you in, but she died. They chose to keep you, knowing nothing of her people."

"My ears." She touched the slight uptilting of her right ear.

"They have started to change."

Estellyn wanted to argue, but she knew Lystra told

the truth. "Who is my father?"

"I have not seen an answer to that question. Even as an Elf, you are different. To see a unicorn is rare, yet you have called them to you as they have called you to them."

"Jeremian says there will be a foal. Did the goblin know? Did it want them for that?"

"You ask uneasy questions. When did you see a pair?"

"Almost a week ago. The goblin followed them. I drove it away."

"How?"

"With the staff."

"Your walking stick?"

"Astebery gave it to me. I brought it to Jeremian because words are written in the wood, and I can't read. But his life was threatened, and we've run. There hasn't been time."

"Let me see." Lystra held out her hand. She rubbed her fingers along the string of symbols. "This is more than I thought. In ancient days, far away in fair lands, grew the great tree. It was said to be harder than iron and the fruit it bore sweeter than honey. When that land fell to the wiles of the Dark Lord, the tree produced five staffs for the councilors of the wise. This is one of theirs."

"What does that mean?"

Lystra peered at her. "I don't know."

Twelve

Riven wandered blindly for more than a day. Color beat against his eyes. The trees were green, but different than the green of the brush. Grasses swayed in their own shade of green, and there was heather with its hint of purple. He noticed a hundred different hues and still more as he staggered on. Red made him choke on his breath. It was not the fiery color of flames, this red shone with light and smelled sweet. He fell to his knees, wanting to crush the life between his hands but afraid to touch it.

He pulled himself up and continued. A short while later, trees thinned, and a grassy hill rose toward the east. Tiny yellow flowers covered the hill. For some reason he did not understand, he pulled his shoes from his feet and stepped forward. Cool soft touched his skin. A sound he'd never heard came from him. Puzzled, he walked further. Light poured over him from above. The ground covering tickled his skin. He became drunk with sensation. He cheeks dampened even though he felt free and something he had no words to describe. He fell backward, arms spread out, face to the sky. A sweet smell from the flowers surrounded him. He sighed and closed his eyes. An unusual expression was on his face, he could feel. He'd seen it on others but hadn't understood until now. It welled up from within and marked his face. He smiled.

~

Estellyn and Jeremian frowned.

"Is it a trap?"

"What is he doing?"

Their low voices mingled. The man they knew to be an evil emissary of the Dark Lord sat up with the smile still on his face. It wasn't a forced or faked smile, but rather contented. They heard him laugh again. A strange sound as though he couldn't keep himself from it yet had no idea what or why.

Estellyn gripped the staff tighter. "It's the same man, I would swear to it, but he's as unlike himself as ever a stranger could be."

"We should leave."

"And what? Keep a vigil by day and night? We have him unawares now. The moment he turns away…"

He sighed. "We open ourselves to attack. Better we strike here." Jeremian reached for his sword.

Estellyn stopped him with a hand on his arm. "Be ready but don't draw. There is too much a difference for this not to be significant."

He agreed, keeping his sword sheathed with his hand resting on the hilt. They moved out from the protection of the trees.

He noticed them but didn't move. Jeremian and Estellyn came close enough to kick him if need be. She cleared her throat. "Why have you come here?"

"I don't know. I have no memory of seeking this place." His eyes that had filled her with fear were now wide and curious. The cold dark had left them. He titled his head. "There is something familiar about you." He pointed at Jeremian. "You as well."

Jeremian stood with his feet apart and his hand still on the hilt of his sword. "You worked the weapon's yard at the king's castle."

"Weapons?"

Jeremian stepped closer. "You plotted to have me killed."

"Killed?" He startled, then his face fell. "There was darkness, lots of gray in a colorless world."

"Are you a servant of the Dark Lord?" Estellyn asked as she pulled Jeremian back.

The stranger furrowed his brows and tilted his head. "The Dark Lord in his Dark Realm sits on a white throne. I don't want to think of him. I don't want to remember."

Jeremian scoffed. "We are to believe you've turned on him?"

He stared at Estellyn. "A healer touched me. I felt heat of the sun and thought I was to burn."

"What do you intend to do now?" She softened her tone.

He fell back onto the grass as though he didn't know what to answer.

Jeremian tugged her back toward the trees. He stopped, glanced at the stranger. "What game does he play?"

"What makes you think it's a game? Can the servant of the Dark Lord feign delight in something good?"

"Send him to your father to work on the farm. See if he is changed."

Estellyn chewed her lower lip. "He is caught up in this adventure as we are, whether for good or ill. Perhaps Astebery can tell for certain."

Jeremian leaned closer. "You can't take him to see a unicorn," he hissed. "Sacred animals. You would expose them to evil?"

"Lystra, then."

"Are Elves to be trusted?"

"She's the only one I know."

They both turned as the stranger stood and stretched.

~

"There is too much we don't know." Jeremian paced, careful to keep an eye on Riven. "My brothers return to the castle for the queen's birth honoring. Duncan knowns the libraries. There may be knowledge or wisdom written in one of the old tomes. He may be able to help us."

Estellyn lifted a brow. "You want to tell them now?"

"Not everything." He frowned. "Riven helps trap the soldiers planning to kill me."

"What do I do?"

His grin seemed a bit sheepish. "If this wasn't a family gathering, I would invite you to join us."

"The farmhouse is too far away."

"Remain in Allington. We plan our next steps."

"We have to find out if the Dark Lord plans to attack Overworld."

"There is a seer."

"The one who warned of your brother's death?"

"No, he was in Hoff. The seer of Allington is a woman. Might not be the best plan," Jeremian admitted, "but I don't know what else to do."

"Attending your mother's birth honoring is important. If there are to be darker days coming, a present celebration is in order." She nodded as though determining for them all. "We return to Allington."

Riven blinked. "You want me to go with you?"

Jeremian frowned. "Consider it a test to see what has changed in you. Did you plot with soldiers to harm me?"

Riven tilted his head. "They wanted you dead and I would provide access to a treasure room to pay them for the deed."

Jeremian hissed. "You remember well."

"I don't know why that is no longer on my heart."

"Perhaps he should stay with me," Estellyn wondered.

"No." Jeremian's reply came swift. "Let him prove himself. He will return to the barracks."

Thirteen

Riven remained quiet most of the journey back to Allington. Bursts of color fascinated him. Estellyn finally pulled a yellow flower from a vine and handed it to him. "You should smell it."

"Do colors have smells?"

She laughed. "Flowers have smells. Well, I guess most everything has smell. Flowers smell sweet."

Jeremian rolled his eyes. "Smell yourself after a day running drills in the fields and you'll understand many things do not smell sweet."

The market was in high swing when they arrived. "Do you know how to return to your barracks from here?" Jeremian asked.

Riven glanced around and nodded.

"Good. Find the soldiers and report them to one of the captains."

Riven agreed.

Estellyn felt uncertain about them all going different ways. "Where should we meet tomorrow?"

"The boarding house on High Street has a garden area. We can meet there after the noon hour."

Estellyn managed to acquire a room at the same

boarding house after leaving the others. From her window, she could see across the city. The road leading to the castle was behind her. Uneasiness gripped her, but everything seemed as it should. Then why the feel of evil intent lurking in the shadows? Perhaps a visit to the seer could be useful. She found her way to the kitchen. "There's an old seer," she started to ask the woman rolling dough.

"Maisie?" She didn't stop rolling the dough across a wood board. "She don't like to be bothered by people."

"Unless there is a purpose to it." An old woman stood in the open door leading out to a plot of vegetables.

"Upon my heart," the cook pressed a doughy hand against her chest. "What are you doing here?"

Maisie blinked. "I've come to speak with the child." She waved for Estellyn to join her outside.

The cook looked from Maisie to Estellyn. Estellyn shrugged. "Someone must have already told her I wanted to meet."

Maisie sat on a bench beside a row of greens. "I wasn't sure you would return to Allington."

Estellyn sat beside her. "I thought seers knew things."

"We have visions, wisdom that can help. You're being here is not good, but I cannot tell you where you should go."

"What did you want to tell me?"

Maisie stood and turned around. When Estellyn stood beside her, they could see towers of the castle above the boarding house.

Maisie sighed. "Darkness has come. Death is here for the family of the king."

Estellyn started. "Jeremian?"

"And his brothers."

Estellyn looked at Maisie. "The seer in Hoff told Jeremian his brother would die. That is why he sought for the unicorn."

Maisie closed her eyes. "All I see is blood and death, and deep waters filled with evil things."

"Can we stop it? Change what is to happen?"

"You will be in that dark place, but I cannot see what happens to you there."

"Is there nothing of hope you can give us?"

"Child," Maisie sounded surprised. "You are hope. It is not only your name, but who you are. You will be in the dark place, but it will not consume you. I do not know if you will be able to save others." She was silent a moment. "When you meet the seer of Hoff, he may have a different vision for you."

Estellyn frowned. "I am not going to Hoff."

Maisie grinned but said nothing further. She returned to the bench. Estellyn sat beside her for a few moments. The noise of people was different than what she knew living on the farm. Yet, there was comfort in the day-to-day actions of others. It was a peaceful day. She breathed it in.

Maisie eventually patted Estellyn's knee. "Best to get to work, child. I will stay here for you."

~

Work first meant getting the attention of Riven and Jeremian. There was no easy way for her to get into the castle, so she searched for Riven on the training fields. When he finished pacing a young solider with horrible aim, she tossed a rock at his shoulder. He turned sharply. Estellyn was surprised to see fear on him before he noticed her. She waved for him to join her under the trees. Riven checked around him before jogging toward her. He stood almost a head taller, she noticed as he stood in front of her.

"We need to get Jeremian from the castle."

"How do we do that?"

"I have no reason to go inside, but I overheard you say you can get into treasure rooms. That could be our way in."

"And then what? How do we find him?"

Estellyn breathed. "There must be a way." She peered across the field. "Have you seen him or any of his brothers training today?"

He shrugged. "Snechtal works with one of the captains."

Estellyn thought for a moment. "Ask if he will meet with me. I have a request of him."

Riven looked doubtful. "I can try."

Estellyn paced through the trees as she waited for Riven to return, with or without another prince. She tried to flatten wrinkles in her split skirt. She wasn't quite dressed the way one would when wanting an audience with a royal. Jeremian never made her feel as less of a person. What would his brother do? She walked more. It was sometime later when she heard others approaching. Riven was followed by a slightly older man with red hair. His face resembled Jeremian.

He hesitated when he saw her. "What is this?" With a hand on the hilt of his sword, he took as step back.

"Wait, please," Estellyn asked as she held up her hand. "I need to speak with Jeremian."

He frowned. "Ask for him at the gate."

She laughed. "Their reaction would be much like yours. Please, it is important. Tell him Estellyn is here and needs to see him, if only for a moment."

"You are friends with my brother?"

"I am." She lifted her chin. "I practiced movements with a sword, and he decided to butt in and help."

"Can't blame him wanting to help a pretty girl. I will mention your name. If he is favorable, I'll send him to you." He gave a tight bow and left.

"What do you want me to do?" Riven asked.

"Prepare a travel pack. We must leave tonight. Wait for us in the garden at the boarding house."

~

This time, the wait took longer. Snechtal could have ignored her. She studied the side of the castle she could see from the training field. How could she tell if any of the windows belonged to the royal family? Would there be another way to find Jeremian? Disguise herself as a scullery maid?

"What are you doing here?" Jeremian approached without her notice.

She whirled around. "You came!" She wanted to hug him but kept her distance.

"Snechtal thinks I have a secret romance. He's going to hold it over me for some time."

Estellyn felt her spirits droop. "Not if what the seer told me is true."

"What do you mean? You went to her?"

"She came to me. You and your brothers are in danger."

"But how?"

"I don't know. You need to leave tonight. Find a way to warn the others."

"Tonight, is the birth honoring of the queen. Everything has been well guarded."

"Unless someone you trust has betrayed you all."

He shook his head. "Where are we to go?"

"I think we should go to Hoth. The woman I met today said the seer of Hoth may give us more information. Better direction." Estellyn stood in front of Jeremian. "I'm sorry. I know how important this evening is."

Jeremian stared for a moment before nodding. "I cannot miss the celebration, but I will meet you at the boarding house directly after. There is enough moon tonight we can travel some way in the dark." He turned, then glanced at her again. "Riven? What of him?"

"He will wait for you as well. We go together."

"Of all I know, he is the most likely to betray us."

"Which is why keeping him with us is better." Estellyn breathed as Jeremian returned to the castle. She closed her eyes. Her heart remained unsettled.

91

Book 2: The Growing Darkness

Fourteen

A week before the queen's birth honoring, Captain Grilick turned from the familiar road passing through Allington into the woods. Hidden among the trees, he waited. No one followed. He continued his journey southeast, into the wildlands. He followed a trail, though none who did not know it would see it as such. The sun had set and several hours into the night he arrived at the cave. Within it was a shallow stream and a grassy pad. Beyond that, another tunnel lead deeper into the earth, to the Dark Realm.

"Only a fool or one summoned would take this path," a garbled voice of a sentry stopped him.

Grilick kept one hand on the hilt of his sword and carried a lantern in the other. "I am summoned. I have news for Lord Morgeth."

"Then you best move. He is not a patient master."

How the Dark Realm came to be, Grilick knew not. What he'd seen of it brought to mind an underground palace, much larger than the House of Taighlais. Once he entered the main hallway, he had no further use for the lantern. He placed it at the mouth of the path he'd need to take to return to Overworld. He was familiar enough with the layout of the Dark Realm to get himself to the Chamber of Rule. Stone pillars, likely carved by dwarves, supported the roof of the cave further than could be seen. Open fires and lanterns hanging on the walls provided ample light and warmth against the natural cold of the stone. From where he entered, the royal seat was to his right. There was an incline, a step, and then chairs arranged in a half circle, the central one clearly greater than the others. A pale stone throne formed with pillars surrounded a seat. Though they were far underground, cathedral-like windows behind the platform were lit, causing a glimmer in the rock of the chair. The one who sat upon it was more beautiful and terrible to behold.

"Lord Morgeth," Grilick rubbed a thick scar over his left eyebrow as he bowed before the carved throne.

Morgeth crossed one leg over the other and tapped his fingers on his knee. "I have waited too long for you, Grilick."

Grilick swallowed. The relaxed image of Lord Morgeth did not calm his fears. "I searched the palace and the grounds repeatedly. There remains no sign of your servant."

"Is he dead?"

Grilick blinked. "How would I… No mention has been made. I saw the princes at meals. Only they would have the means to have someone killed."

"The princes are of the royal house of Taighlais?"

He nodded slowly. "They have been caretakers of Overworld time out of mind."

"Because they carry blood of the Elven realm."

"Myths and legends, my lord." Grilick scoffed.

Morgeth flew from his seat to strike Grilick's

cheek. "Am I not able to sense my own?"

Grilick stumbled back. "My apologies. Of course. I always thought those tales to be childish stories."

"There is truth in them." Morgeth stepped forward, causing Grilick to move further away. Morgeth continued. "I have heard the blood of fairy can quicken the molting process of goblins. How many princes are there?"

"Seven, my lord, but I doubt…"

"I do not. I will have those seven brothers." He returned to his chair, swept his robes so as to sit.

"All of them? What of the line of the king?" Grilick gulped, hands shaking.

Morgeth scoffed. "Am I not building an army to destroy the house of Taighlais? They need no further ascension to the throne." He strode to Grilick and took him by the throat. "I will be your king. Those creatures from the Maker will be destroyed. I will be your king and your god. Get me your princes so I may spill their blood at the pools."

Eyes bulging, he nodded. "Yes, my lord."

Fifteen

"It's the queen's birthday. Of course, we need to be there," Olith, third son of King Aeoloch Fengormeth, grabbed his younger brother, Snechtal.

Snechtal jerked free. 'I don't need you to remind me. Find that runt, Jeremian. If any of us are missing, it will be him."

"That is the truth," Gail said as she leaned against her husband.

Olith nodded. "I already sent his servant to search him out. Father is determined to have all of us present."

Snechtal chuckled. "Is that why he had Lindulf and Duncan brought home early? They voiced their displeasure loudly."

"It is not your place, sire, to repeat what other princelings have spoken," Grilick joined them, his face stern.

Snechtal released Gail. "Sir," he acknowledged the reprimand by lowering his eyes to the ground.

"When the sun touches the tower, you are in the main dining hall. King Aeoloch has ordered the grand table be set for the occasion."

"Bother," Orlith grinned. "We'll have to use our

best manners. Mother will think she's raised a pack of wolves."

Grilick pressed his hand on Orlich's shoulder. "You look more and more like your father every time I see you."

"Aeol is still the future king. I get the pleasure of my father's good name with none of the responsibility."

Snechtal rolled his eyes. "Away with you." He took Gail's hand. "We will be there at the appointed time."

Grilick watched them disperse in different directions. He remembered when they had been halflings, running toward whatever the next moment held. He closed his mind against such thoughts. They would soon be dead. All of them.

~

"Ah, my poor son," Queen Eilidh Lilliasing touched a lock of Jeremian's dark hair. "I ran out of red by the time you came along." She narrowed her eyes when she noticed a lock of silver had grown. "What is this? You are too young to have the mark of an aged man."

Jeremian grinned and kissed her cheek. "I must have been touched by a fairy in the night. Besides, it is a good thing to stand out from my brothers."

Edmund pushed him. "There was no need for another."

The queen squeezed Jeremian's hand before letting him go and turning to another son. "He is nearly ten years your junior…"

He moved before listening to more of her admonishment to Edmund. He took his seat at the end of the table, beside Lindulf.

"Villagers in the western ridge swore that some

have seen it." Lindulf leaned in as he talked.

"Seen what?" Jeremian asked as he plopped in the chair beside him.

Lindulf's brown eyes gleamed. "A unicorn."

Jeremian glanced at Duncan then back to Lindulf. "Is that possible?" They wouldn't believe him if he told them of his own encounter.

Duncan frowned. "Lore does exist in the libraries, but that was ages ago. Can they still exist today?"

"They are agents of good sent by the Maker, are they not? To watch over our lands?"

"Watch for what?" Lindulf laughed. "I never heard stories of unicorns from my nursery pap. What manner of old woman did they find for you?"

Jeremian protested. "Mistress Mirren wasn't that old a pap."

Lindulf shook his head. "She filled your mind with stories."

Duncan protested. "Stories have meaning, they are not mere nonsense."

"Of course, you would say that; you spend more time among dusty words than in the real world."

He shrugged. "I like it there."

Jeremian tapped his fork on his plate to turn the conversation back where he wanted it. "What did villagers say about a unicorn?"

"Only that it was seen up on the ridge. From a distance. They could easily have been mistaken."

But they weren't, Jeremian stared at his plate. *I am chosen as a champion, even better than being a hero.* He did not voice his thoughts, knowing the scorn he would receive.

Much later, after a grand meal, Grilick himself

brought a round of drinks for a final toast with the queen.

King Aeoloch stood. "Master Grilick, this is an unusual honor."

Grilick bowed his head. "Lord Majesty, on my most recent travel to the eastern woods, I was gifted with a mead of the Rowans. In honor of the queen this evening, I offer it to you."

King Aeoloch nodded. "May you have blessing upon blessing, my friend." He took the first glass.

Grilick walked around the table. Queen Eilidh accepted the glass inlaid with green gems. Prince Aeol sat beside her. Snechtal took two, offering one to Gail. Lindulf, Duncan, and Jeremian accepted theirs, then he reached Olith and Edmund on the other side of the table. He bowed to them all and backed away.

King Aeoloch raised his glass. "There is beauty in more than your face, and honor beyond that of sons. May the blessing of the Maker ever keep you."

"Here, here," a chorus of agreement followed before everyone drank from their cup. King Aeoloch kissed the queen's forehead before sitting down.

Jeremian allowed only a touch of the liquor in his mouth to honor his father's toast. Plans for the night required an alertness that would be tainted if he were to drink more.

~

He dismissed his servant the moment he returned to his rooms. "Be at peace. The hour is late, and I have no further need for your assistance this evening." The slightly older man thanked him for his kindness and left. Jeremian found a pack in his wardrobe and filled it with clothing, a sleeping pad, and blanket. But the top would not close. He pulled a heavy cape from its hook. "This will do." He removed the blanket and closed the pack.

He draped a second, smaller bag across his chest. He used the back steps to the kitchen. Bread, meat pies, a flask of wine and a bag of water fit in the bag. When he stepped through the kitchen door into the herb garden, he wrapped the thick cape around him and secured it at his throat. Stars gleamed overhead. He wore his sword at his side. What else did he require? When nothing came to mind, he stole across the garden, through the gate, and into the field. All was quiet as he disappeared into the dark.

LAURIE LEE

Sixteen

Grilick unlocked the cellar door.

A goblin grunted. "You mean to keep us here all night to be picked off by soldiers when the sun rises?" It hissed and gurgled.

"Silence," Grilick checked behind him, but there was no one. "This is not a safe endeavor, and I cannot hold back an attack if your presence is made known." He narrowed his lips. "They are sleeping. Take only the princes."

It lifted a leather bag. "The master will have them all when the time comes."

"That time is not today."

Nearly twenty goblins followed him from the cellars to the sleeping quarters. Guards had been sent on fool errands for the night. The first room they reached was Edmunds. His red hair stood out against the white bedclothes. He did not wake as a pair of goblins worked him into a bag. They threw him over a shoulder and returned to the basement to wait.

It wasn't until they reached Jeremian's rooms that Grilick discovered his problem.

"Where is he?" The lead goblin snarled.

"If he went anywhere else, the drug would have knocked him out. There's no telling where he might be." Grilick checked the other rooms anyway. "He is not here."

"Where do you suggest we look?"

"I don't know."

"Lord Morgeth does not do well with disappointment." The goblin hissed.

"I am aware," Grilick growled. "Take the others. When I find him myself, I will bring him."

~

"Put them in cells, not near each other. The ritual will take place at the rising of the next new moon, whether we have all seven or not."

Aeol pressed his nails into his hands in an attempt to clear the fog from his mind. The bag around him stank, as though it had carried dead things. Who spoke? What ritual did he mean?

Getting tossed over someone's shoulder jarred him, but he let his body dangle. They were moving. Could any of the others be awake? He heard nothing. They moved downstairs. Goblins talked, but he couldn't understand what they said. Sometime later, he was dropped on a hard floor, his head reeling as it struck. Someone pulled at the ties of the bag. He feigned unconsciousness as he was pushed and turned to pull the bag off. It was when his arms were released, he jumped up and grabbed the goblin, twisting its head before it could push him away or call an alarm. He let the dead body drop to the floor and staggered against the wall. The stench of the dungeon was as bad as the bag. He rubbed his face to clear more of the fog. Had someone drugged him? Where were the others?

He pushed the body over. After a thorough check, he found a blade. It was wide and rudimentary, but it would do. There were more creatures in the hallway. A few carried bags over their shoulders. His brothers?

He thought he followed quietly, but one of the goblins turned on him. "Where do you think you're going?"

Before he could raise his sword, another goblin tore open a bag. He pulled Snechtal by the hair, holding his head with a blade at his throat. "You want him to die here?"

"Return to your cell," the other snarled at him.

Aeol shook. "What do you want with us?"

The goblin shook Snechtal, who's eyes twitched.

Aeol dropped the sword, its clang a solemn toll through the dungeon.

"Go."

He couldn't think of what else to do. He returned to the cell and pulled the dead goblin out by the feet. Three of them watched. The middle one stepped over and slammed his fist against Aeol's head. He fell back.

"Enough," someone else growled.

Aeol heard the door slam and a lock turn.

LAURIE LEE

Seventeen

Morgeth felt power growing within him, yet something hindered it's working. Two things. The youngest prince for one. The full strength of Elvish blood could only be achieved with all seven sons. With the new moon rising in a week, there was little time to find the wayward princeling. Grilick best not fail him. But more than his need to find the prince, the young woman who invaded his realm for a moment, weighed more and more on his mind. What had happened to Riven and his search for the girl? Why did she draw his attention?

"Orlin," Morgeth considered the captain of mercenaries pledged to his will. A network of spies spread across Overworld would be more useful than sending more of his own minions to search blindly. He motioned for one of the attendants standing near the door. "Send me Orlin."

Unlike the unnatural twisting of goblins, Orlin's gravelly face came as a result of hard living with a hardened heart. "Lord Morgeth, I did not anticipate your requiring me so soon. Our pact was for six months hence."

"Am I interrupting something?"

"Just what little pleasure I can afford."

"Achieve this favor for me and I will be certain to provide you the means for whatever pleasure you desire."

Orlin fixed himself a glass of wine from a side table. "What manner of favor do you ask?"

"I want someone found. You have a network of mercenaries. Find me a girl."

Orlin paused with the goblet almost touching his lips. "A girl?"

"Her name is Estellyn. I do not know of what family. My servant, Riven, tracked her but he has disappeared through some foul turn. Provide me her accurate whereabouts and I will repay you richly."

"Find her?" He took a drink. "You don't want us to bring her to you?"

Morgeth stared at Orlin. "If you can guarantee she will be brought unharmed and unspoiled."

He shrugged. "Shouldn't be a problem."

"Failure to do so would bring unmitigated pain and suffering for a lifetime." Morgeth stepped closer. "Do you doubt me?"

Orlin swallowed. "I believe you. I will treat her better than my own daughter. We will find her and bring her to you."

~

The cold night was not dispersed by lanterns hanging in the boarding house garden. Strange shadows seemed to lurch beyond the hedges. Estellyn wrapped her arms around herself, pacing along the walkways. Riven sat on a bench, leaning against the outer wall of the house. Though she passed him a few times, he said nothing. Rustling leaves announced someone moving toward them. She turned as Jeremian stepped through an arch of morning glory

He acknowledged her and noticed Riven as well. "This evening seems restless, though I see no one on the streets."

"There is a foul smell. I say we take the back garden gate and stay among the trees."

Jeremian adjusted his pack. "We head for Hoth? It will take us a week walking if the weather remains fair."

She nodded as Riven stood silently.

Jeremian yawned and shook his head.

Estellyn grinned. "Do you need a nap before we go?"

He grunted. "Come on."

They didn't get far from Allington before Jeremian's stumbling forced them to stop. "I don't understand." Jeremian rubbed his hand across his face.

"I hope you aren't getting sick." Estellyn peered at the trees surrounding them. "Might as well stop here. The pines can be used beneath our sleeping mats."

"We haven't gone far at all."

Estellyn placed her hand on his arm. "You are in no shape to continue tonight. Get settled. Riven and I can set up camp."

A while later, Riven crouched across the fire from Estellyn. "I don't think he's joining us for a meal."

A fire crackled in the dark as a stew provided by her boarding host bubbled in a small pot. "Does he seem feverish? Ill?" Estellyn asked as she stirred.

He frowned. "I felt no heat coming off him. How else would you tell?"

She broke a bit of brown bread from a loaf and handed it to Riven.

He sniffed it.

Estellyn dipped hers in the stew. "It's safe to eat."

Riven hung his head. "There are so many smells in this world. How do they not overwhelm?"

She tilted her head. "Could you not smell… before?"

He shrugged. "All I remember is dull and flat." He glanced around what could be seen by the firelight and overhead moon. "Nothing alive, the way this is." He bent his head as though embarrassed by his mutterings.

"What about before you lived in the Dark Realm?"

He furrowed his brows as he frowned. "I never knew anything else." His eyes gleamed when he looked at her. "I'm not like you or the prince." He tapped his chest. "A foul beast disguised for evil purpose."

Estellyn leaned forward to touch his hand. "I don't know about foul beasts and how they come to be, but there is more to you than you perceive."

He sighed. "I wish that were true, but I have no memory of anything else."

"Maybe someday you'll learn otherwise. For now, look forward. Make fresh memories."

"With sunlight and color?" There was an unusual sparkle in him before his face saddened.

Estellyn poured stew into a bowl for Riven, and then for herself. With focus shifting to their food, they ate in silence. The anxiety that gripped her in the garden in Allington faded, though didn't quite dissipate completely.

~

The sight of an inn where they could have a real meal, get washed, even sleep in a true bed brought tears to Estellyn's eyes. Days on dusty trails marred by rain left her weary and disheartened. Traveling across country through woods and fields to keep from the main roads differed from the trails through highlands.

Jeremian sighed. "We shouldn't."

She shook her head. "We should. We can't arrive in Hoff looking like vagabonds. As we get closer to town, won't we see more villages and travelers? We can take to the main road."

Riven waited between them, silent as usual, though he did watch the movement of people around the large building.

Jeremian thinned his lips but motioned toward the inn. Estellyn's smile made him blink.

~

As they waited to speak with the innkeeper, Estellyn caught sight of a small group of travelers. The members were tall and slender. Their clothing were deep russet colors of fall in styles that were different than that with which she was familiar. Long braids of hair revealed their pointed ears. She almost touched her own. A man caught her staring at them. The deep blue of his gaze held her for a moment.

Jeremian touched her arm. "Estellyn?"

She had a feeling he'd been talking to her, but her attention had been elsewhere. "I'm sorry. Never seen Elves like them before."

Jeremian glanced over her shoulder. "It is rare to encounter Elvish travelers, but not unheard of. The northern clans tend to keep to their lands. We can acquire beds in the rafter dorms."

Estellyn grinned. "You didn't reveal your identity."

He frowned. "I do not think that would be prudent."

She agreed. Before entering the inn, Estellyn peered across the yard. The Elvish travelers had gone.

~

Orlin rarely trusted to fortune, but upon hearing the name Estellyn, he turned to study the young woman. The grime of travel did not hide her features. This was whom he sought. He motioned his crew to join him.

Dresda wrapped her arm around him. "Have your eyes on a dainty already?"

"This one is a commission."

"Who?" She searched the mulling travelers as his other men joined them.

"The girl. She just entered with two companions."

"A trio? I'm certain we can have a bit of fun."

Orlin gripped her arm as he stared at each of his men. "No one is to lay a finger on her beyond capture. She is for Lord Morgeth. No harm is to befall her."

At the name of the lord of the Dark Realm, the others silenced and nodded. He kissed Dresda to make up for his rough handling. She didn't seem to mind either. He gave her a slight push. "Follow her. We will find a way to trap her alone."

"What of her companions?" Another man grunted.

"Lord Morgeth wants her. This prize is valuable. We lack time to make prey of the others."

Dresda pulled the strap of her blouse, tightening it so her shoulder was no longer exposed. "I will make nice with the girl." Her eyes darkened. "I was once young, like her. I think I know what will attract her interest."

~

The rafter dorm for female travelers had two rows of beds, each bed separated by a curtain hung from a ceiling beam. The beds were simple wood structures with mattresses made of course material but well-stuffed.

"Don't leave nothing."

Estellyn jerked around. An older woman with dark straggly hair smiled at her. Estellyn grinned. "I wasn't planning to."

"Put your marker on the bed, especially if this is the one you want." She tilted her head. "Haven't seen you at any of the travel inns."

"I'm here with my brothers. They decided this would be preferred to another campsite."

"Are you meeting them in the pub?"

"I wanted a fresher in the bath house." She sighed. "Feels good to be clean."

At that, the woman chuckled, tugging on her dirty blouse. "Traveling will do this to you. I'm on the way myself, although..." she glanced at the others in the dormer, but no one paid them any attention. "I have a box I didn't tell my husband about. He wanted me to leave a cat and her three kittens. How was I supposed to do that?" She pulled a napkin and showed Estellyn tidbits of chicken and ham she'd saved. "On my way to feed them. Going to pilfer a bit of cream for the wee ones. Don't suppose you'd care to help? You're small enough to get in and out of the kitchens unnoticed."

Estellyn chewed her lip. Kittens? Would be fun to peek. What harm could it do? She grinned and nodded. "I can help." She picked up her bag and followed the stranger downstairs.

Before they reached the entrance, Estellyn heard her name. She turned and waved at Jeremian.

He weaved through the crowd. "We have a table."

Estellyn handed him her bag and walking stick. "I'm going to help snag a little cream for some kittens."

She motioned toward the other woman. "We'll be right back."

Jeremian stretched out his arm to keep her from leaving. "What do you mean?"

"Going to make a quick trip to the barn. We'll be fine. I'll meet you at the table. Is that Riven in the back corner?"

"I don't think it's a good idea." Jeremian frowned.

Estellyn matched the irritated look on his face. "We chose to stop, so we're here. With this many people around, what harm is there in a trip to the barn? I'll be fine."

Her words proved to be an alarming falsehood.

Giggles from the older woman caused Estellyn to giggle as they peered through an outside doorway into the kitchen. Workers bustled around a wide stove. Estellyn covered her mouth to stop any noise from alerting their presence. The woman nudged her and pointed to a silver pitcher. Estellyn nodded. No one seemed to be in that area.

The woman handed her a mug with a chip broken out of the lip. "Dip this. At least half should do."

It proved easier than she thought. Dart in, dart out, then the two of them were hurrying across the darkened yard.

"I can't believe we did it." She handed the cup to the woman and wiped her fingers against her cape. "Although I'm sure you could have asked."

"Wouldn't have been nearly as much fun, would it?" She winked. "Hurry, they still have the lights on." She headed toward the barn.

The structure was much larger than any on the family farm, Estellyn thought. They steered toward the area where traveler coaches were stored, and horses tended. She gazed at a thick chestnut stallion taller than herself. Its intelligent eyes put her in mind of Astebery. How was the unicorn?

"That was easier than I imagined."

Estellyn whirled at the sound of a man's voice. The woman hung against an older man with a balding head, then allowed her hands to fall away as he moved forward. Estellyn backed up a step, but someone took her from behind. The older man gripped her chin and moved her head back and forth so he could examine her. "You are his prize. I don't envy you that." His eyes narrowed. "There's something about you..." Then, as though releasing temptation, he removed his hold and stepped back. He motioned to the cart with his head.

"Why are you doing this?" Estellyn struggled against the man holding her. He tightened his grip, making her whimper.

The older man snarled at her. "You were with two men earlier."

"Her brothers," the woman interjected.

"Your brothers." The older man grinned. "I'll kill them if you fight. What part would you like me to bring you for proof?"

Estellyn let herself be pushed into the cart. A door closed, locking her in. Fear chilled her as she felt the wagon move moments later. She pulled the clasp from her cape and shoved it through the bars in the door. Would Jeremian or Riven find it? Even if they did, how could they follow?

~

Jeremian returned to the table carrying Estellyn's stuff. Riven raised a brow. "What is she doing?"

"Finding trouble, I'm afraid." He hesitated. The scent of food at another table made his mouth water, but a stronger caution kept him standing.

Riven rose to his feet. "You think she's in danger?"

He nodded. "But she will not be happy if we follow her."

Riven collected his pack. "Does it matter?"

"No." They hurried through the pub into the yard. No one was around, but lights flickered in the barn. They went towards it. They had just stepped through an opening for wagons when someone shouted. "Out of the way, fools."

They scrambled from the path of a horse and wagon and its driver. Jeremian shook his head, then turned his attention to finding Estellyn.

Riven kept his focus on the escaping wagon.

Jeremian found him standing in the same spot when he returned. "She's not here."

Riven had his hands at his side but held them in tight fists. "Something fell from the back of the wagon."

"Is it important?" Jeremian looked into the night but couldn't see anything.

Riven nodded. "Go toward the green bush. I will tell you when you should see something."

Something was there. It glimmered and caused Jeremian's body to turn cold. He'd last seen the silver clasp with etched flowers on Estellyn's cape. He never asked how she came by it, though it seemed unusual for a farmer's daughter. He crouched and wrapped his hand around it.

Riven stood beside him. "He has her."

Jeremian stood. "Who?"

"Lord Morgeth."

The chill in his body deepened. "How could you know that?"

"I am of the Dark Realm. The scent of it lingers in the air."

~

Estellyn lay on the floor of the wagon where managing bumps of the uneven path proved less painful. Even when they stopped, she had no time to collect herself before the small door opened and rough hands pulled her. They were in a cave, not a place she wanted to be. Copying movements she'd seen soldiers using in the palace yard, she knocked her head against one of her captors. Pain radiated from the impact, but he seemed more dazed than she, staggering back and dropping to the ground.

"Don't touch her," one of the men growled, but it was too late. Another captor slammed something on the side of her head, and she dropped into darkness.

Eighteen

Lord Morgeth paced before the great fire whose flames drew from the deepest recesses of the Dark Realm. "Who is this girl that I should feel her presence?"

"Have you not guessed?" A shadow appeared like smoke from the fire with a thousand voices speaking as one.

Memory hovered of a woman long gone.

"The woman whom you took, Myrina, had a child."

"My child?"

"No. The girl is not of your blood. Myrina gave her life that she might live."

"I will have her."

"You must turn her first. She is young. Woo her. Tempt her with riches and beauty. Make her one of us." The shadow dissipated, the voices fading until only the crackling fire could be heard.

Light glimmered in his eyes. She would turn or she would die. He would not make the same mistake he'd made with Myrina.

~

Darkness surrounded her. Estellyn pushed herself into a sitting position. Pain radiated from her head. She touched the area, which didn't help. She rested her head in her arms crossed over her knees. Breathing the air didn't alleviate her sense of nausea. She closed her eyes and forced herself to attend to her surroundings. Water dripped into a puddle. Her ears rang with silence, but there was something more. A rumble vibrated through the ground. She swallowed. Her throat cracked from dryness. She reached her hand to the left and felt a cold splash on her palm. She licked the water. Its bitter taste didn't help her stomach, but it was wet. She reached for more drops.

A door opened. The sound of it shouted through the empty hall. Estellyn waited, but nothing more happened. Opening her eyes, she looked up. All remained in darkness, but air moved where there had been nothing. Still, she waited. How much time passed, she couldn't tell. Nothing else could be heard. She stood, leaning against the wall as her head swam. She bit down on her lip, using the pain to focus. She moved forward.

One step at a time, she felt the space in front of her before shuffling then reaching out to take another step. She gauged the location of the sound of the door and tried to move toward it.

Cold seeped into her bones. Beyond the doorway was pale. It didn't even seem like light, just a lessoning of the dark, making it possible to see the outline of the door. She had a direction to go. Fear almost kept her back, but she forced her feet to move in the direction of the hall.

She paused before crossing the threshold. Heart pounding, she peeked through. Stone lined the hallway. Slight movement of air brushed against her, causing the hairs on her arm to shiver. She swallowed, then stepped forward. The hall was vacant. Whomever opened the door was gone.

Her prison remained a black gulf. She had no desire to returned. She moved to the right instead.

~

"You know the Dark Realm."

"Not well. Not with any certainty." Riven rubbed his eyes.

Jeremian grabbed his collar. "What do you think they'll do to her? There are fates worse than death."

"I've lived that life already. I cannot go back."

Jeremian breathed. "We have to rescue her."

Riven's face darkened, and a muscle in his jaw clenched. "We die for her. We mustn't be captured. He would twist our nature. Promise me you will aim an arrow through my heart."

Jeremian trembled. He recognized Riven's fear—knowledge. He released the other man. "I promise. We accept death at all costs not to allow the Dark Lord control of us."

"Where is your courage?"

"It is with my heart. Where do we find an entrance?"

Riven led the way. For two days they walked until Jeremian no longer recognized the land.

"This is it." Riven shivered. They stood at the top of a hill slipping downward toward rock. "We crossed a stream not far behind us. We should fill our waterskins."

"Does it matter?" Jeremian tried not to let the cold gloom impact his courage.

Riven sighed. "There is nothing good in deep places of the world."

The side trip didn't take long. Riven led them along

a narrow path. Old oaks grew tall, their limbs intertwined far above them. Light dimmed. Air grew heavy. A foul stench curled around the path. Jeremian gagged, eyes watering. "Where are we?"

"An entrance where we will go unnoticed."

"You should have warned me."

"Would it have helped?"

Black water flowed from a cave carrying refuse from the Dark Realm. The path they followed, those free of debris, slickened from spray of the river. Jeremian felt his foot slide. Riven grabbed his arm. "You don't want to fall into the water."

Jeremian and swallowed. "No, I do not." He tread carefully until they moved further from the river. The path curved left and downward.

~

Blue light gleamed in one of the rooms along the hallway, drawing Estellyn aside. A table filled with gems and jewels broke the dark. She'd seen jewels before, but never so close, nor filling a room with their own light. She touched one. It felt cold. Most of what covered the table were loose stones, but a few boxes held real jewelry. A necklace with several strands glittered as she lifted it. What would it be to wear such a treasure? The temptation to put it on made her hands shake.

Enchantments. Spells. The sensible part of her mind knew something was amiss. Still, she struggled to let the necklace fall back into the box. She rubbed her hands on the rough material of her tunic. It gave her strength to move on, away from the wealth that could be hers for the taking.

After a time, the hall opened into a cavernous space. Light flickered from a fire far away. A side table with pitchers of water reminded her of thirst. More enchantments. She frowned.

"What do you want?" A voice, deep and pleasant, reached to her from the shadows.

"Have you something to offer?" she asked. Someone she could not see laughed at her small voice in the grand space. She saw no one around her. "These things are meant to captivate and ensnare."

"It is no more than the desires of your heart. You are poor and have longed for things of beauty. You have traveled a great way and thirst."

Estellyn scoffed. "You mean I've been beaten and imprisoned, not traveled."

The man moves closer. "If you were truly imprisoned, you would still be in your cage."

"Isn't this realm a cage?"

"Because I prefer streams of gold flowing through the rock instead of Starlight overhead?"

Estellyn turned. The Elf she saw was both beautiful and terrible. White flesh stood out against the black robes draped over his tall body. Silver hair fell down his back. Something about him reminded her of another.

"What is on your mind?"

She didn't want to say anything but staring into his blue eyes compelled her. "You are like Lystra."

He laughed. "The shield Elf? I am not as foolish as the one who links her life force with another."

"You mean the unicorns?"

"She will die when their life is cut from them."

"Is it so easy to destroy something that is light and love?"

"The unicorns are dumb beasts. Power is not theirs."

"They have enough power to prevent your spilling onto the surface lands. That is what you want, isn't it?"

"Clever girl. I see why you are a chosen champion. Champions will not save them, nor you."

Estellyn grabbed his arm. Her gut clenched at the feel of malice. His mouth twisted with loathing, but she did not release him. In her mind she saw a city burning. A white horse flew with powerful wings as a dragon swooped toward it. He slammed his other fist against her temple, and everything went black.

~

The Dark Realm was like a castle city with large caverns and rooms connected by a labyrinth of halls. Riven led them into narrow halls where the low ceiling caused pain to their heads. Jeremian cursed at the second knock to his forehead. Riven hissed. "Only a fool would make himself known in this place."

"Do you expect me to crawl on my hands and knees?"

"These are service halls. We won't run into guards or any other dwellers."

"How are we going to find Estellyn?" But even as he asked, they spied her hanging over someone shoulder. Riven pushed him into a culvert then pressed into the other side of the hall so they wouldn't be seen.

"Where are they taking her?" Jeremian whispered once they were gone.

~

"Ow," Estellyn groaned as she moved her head. She was in a different room. Though not completely dark, she saw no means of escape. A prior resident lay against the far wall. She scooted across the floor then pushed on the bundle. The material gave way. A hand flopped. Skin and muscle deteriorated to exposed bone. She covered her mouth. One of the fingers had a blue ring. For some reason she couldn't understand, she pulled it from the hand and tucked it in a pocket. She slid away until her back struck a wall. She hugged her knees to her chest and rested her head on them. *Where are you, Jeremian?*

~

"Where are you going?" Jeremian whispered once more as they turned into a dark hallway. "They didn't bring her this way."

"I think I know where they're taking her."

"You think?" Jeremian's whisper turned into a hiss. "We can't afford to lose her."

Riven turned. "I don't want to lose her either, but if we're caught, we're all dead. If you want to take the more direct route, I'll try to free you both." With that, he turned and continued.

Jeremian tapped his foot as he considered the possibilities. Clenching his fists, he followed Riven. If they failed to fine Estellyn…

After some time, Riven stopped without a word. Jeremian didn't need a warning to be silent. The hall opened to a cavernous space. Large domes were set at even intervals across the space. Above them stretched webs, thick webs with dark shadows moving through them. Jeremian clenched his jaw battling his fear of spiders. Riven pointed to a group of them that hovered chattering near a dome. Although he couldn't make distinction more than deep shadows against the pale webs, his imagination flared with thought of long legs spread with hairs and tiny clawed feet prepared to grasp prey. He rubbed his arm. Riven hurried toward the dome.

~

Estellyn heard a faint scrape, then felt something fall nearby. She lifted her head. Something remained in the shadows. Eyes gleamed with cold awareness. She tensed.

~

Riven placed one hand on the dome and followed around it.

"What are you doing?" Jeremian whispered.

"Seeking the latch to open the prison. The spiders will kill if they have the chance."

"Is the latch high or low?"

Riven shrugged, his face tight with fear. "I'm not sure. I never watched it being opened."

"Let's find it." Jeremian winced at the feel of cold stone. Overhead, a shadow moved. Webs vibrated. "Faster!" Jeremian swiped his hand along the face of the rock.

They were more than half around when Riven paused. He moved his hands over the same place, then looked at Jeremian. "I found something."

"Nothing's happening." Jeremian crouched beside him. They pressed on the notched rock, but the dome remained solid.

Screams sounded inside. Heart racing, Jeremian reached higher, following the dent in the rock. His fingers scraped on a latch. "Here," he shouted. A black figure dropped beside him, but he kicked it away. Stone screeched as he pulled the latch upward and a doorway opened.

He moved just in time as a spider hurled toward him from inside. Estellyn held a bone in her hand, screaming as she swung at another. Riven pushed past him, putting himself between Estellyn and another creature attacking. He cried out, then reached over his shoulder to pull a spider off his back. He flung it against the wall and blood spurted.

Jeremian called out. "Use this, Estellyn." He tossed the staff.

As soon as her hand touched wood, light blazed through the dark. Screams lingered in the air as spiders clattered over each other to escape. Though the initial blaze dimmed, it did not go out. Jeremian grabbed her as she swayed. "Are you hurt?"

She breathed, resting her hand against his chest, and looked beyond him to Riven.

Riven glanced around. "We need to go. Now."

"I agree." Jeremian moved with her to the opening. "Are you okay?"

She nodded. "I'm not hurt." Still, she leaned on the staff as they hurried after Riven.

He led them through the labyrinth of halls and tunnels, through caverns where fires belched. Before long, they entered a narrow tunnel heading upward. Riven, leading the way, knocked his head on the ceiling, stumbling to his hands and knees.

Jeremian offered his hand. Riven's pallor seemed heightened, but he said nothing as he continued to lead them. They all had to bend before they reached the end, then the tunnel led to a green field. Most of it remained within the mountain, but on the far side they saw trees and beyond that, a glimpse of day.

Riven stumbled again. This time both Jeremian and Estellyn grabbed hold of him. They pulled him with them toward the open air. Estellyn wanted to set him down as soon as they cleared the cave. Jeremian shook his head.

"We can easily be found. We need to seek shelter for the night."

She glanced around. "I don't know where we are."

Jeremian smiled slightly. "Away from here is a good place to start."

Riven rubbed his head. "We can follow the trail. Should lead to an abandoned farm."

Nineteen

The farm was not so abandoned, Estellyn grunted as she crouched behind a wagon. She glanced at Jeremian. "How about the barn?"

"I'll check. Wait here." He helped Riven lean against the side of the wagon then disappeared.

Estellyn studied Riven. His skin appeared gray. "What happened?"

"I am of the dark and to the dark I return."

She shook her head. "You have not always been, and you no longer are."

"What then? Light has dimmed once more and cold seeps through my joints."

"Lean forward." She pulled without giving an option. Blood streaked the back of his shirt. "You're wounded."

"One of those foul creatures fell on me."

"Lift your shirt." Once more she didn't offer a choice. There were bloody scratches, but also a puncture with streaks of bluish green spreading out. "This is more than a scratch."

Riven sat back with a groan. He twisted his head to look at her. "It bit me?"

She nodded.

He swallowed. "Are you sure?"

"You have a puncture with poison spreading from it."

He closed his eyes. "I always hated those filthy creatures. Where's your sword?"

"No."

"The poison weakens me."

"We'll find a way to stop it."

"You don't understand." He kicked at her. "It's not going to kill me; it'll change me back into a goblin. I can't, I can't sink into that life once more."

"I'm not taking your life."

"You aren't." He grabbed her arm. "You'll be saving me. A clean sweep through the neck. Be sure to cut my head completely from my body."

Estellyn stiffened. "I'm not cutting your head off."

"Where's Jeremian?" He looked around. "Explain to him. He won't mind."

Estellyn frowned but didn't respond. She saw the staff leaning nearby. "I may have something else that will work." She jerked her arm from his grasp then ran to retrieve the staff. "Take your shirt off."

He fumbled with buttons as he shook his head. "What good can a stick do? Think you can beat the poison out of me?"

"Tempting. Lay flat on the ground."

"What's happening?" Jeremian returned.

She nodded at Riven. "The spider bit him. He's been poisoned. Thinks it'll turn him back into a goblin." She stepped beside Riven who lay with his chest on the ground. She saw a strap for a cow and grabbed it. "Here, bite this and hold on to it. This may hurt."

Although she didn't know what to do or say or to expect, the moment Estellyn wrapped her hands around the ancient wood, she felt power. She pressed the edge of the staff against the puncture wound. She didn't speak but pressed down on the wound and thought *destroy poison.*

Riven screamed. Streaks of blue rushed beneath his skin then rose into the air to swirl around the staff. The blue singed and wafted away as ash. His screams stopped and his body dropped, but Estellyn did not release him. Something battled against her. She could not name it. She clenched her jaw, eyes blazing.

"You're going to burn him up from the inside," Jeremian shouted.

Estellyn breathed as a small spider climbed onto the staff. She flung it against the ground and smashed the creature before it could scramble away to hide.

"That was inside him?" Jeremian gasped.

She nodded. "Releasing him before it was drawn out would have bent him to the will of the Dark Lord."

"How did you know to do that?"

They both stared at the thick stick on the ground. She wrapped arms around herself. "I didn't." The buzz of energy still pounded in her blood.

"Do you think he's alive?"

They turned to Riven. Black hair fell against the paleness of his skin. She brushed it away. His skin was warm. He breathed. She felt him stiffen as though memory of her actions still pained him.

He swallowed. "Next time, just take my head."

Twenty

"How does someone enter my realm and leave with my prisoner?" Morgeth stood at the entrance to the spider hives cave. The quietness of his voice bode ill for those around him.

Three goblins standing close moved uncomfortably. "They must have followed somehow." One of them gurgled.

"Who was it?"

The second goblin had a long scar on the side of his face held together by metal strips. "Spiders saw two men, but it was the girl. She made light."

"Made light?" Morgeth glared. "One does not make light, not even an Elf."

"She carried something."

"Not when I saw her. Not when I condemned her to a slow turning."

The first goblin shrugged. "The two men brought it to her."

Morgeth tightened his fists. "Not only does someone come unbidden, but they also brought something of power with them? Who were her companions?"

The three looked at each other but had no answer for him.

Morgeth turned from the cave and walked toward his throne room. "To go unnoticed, yet knowing how to travel through the Dark Realm, he had to be from here." Riven came to mind. How could he have been turned? Killed, yes, that was possible, but released from the hold of the dark lord? As for the other, could Prince Jeremian align with Estellyn? How would the two have met? "Bring me Orlin."

But the mercenary would take time to bring back. There was another source for information. When he arrived at his throne, he motioned for one of the servants. "Have Captain Brocahn join me." It didn't take long for the governor of the military forces to come to the main hall. Captain Brocahn was a man with thick shoulders and a mean face.

"My Lord," he spoke with a gruff voice.

"Have the warden bring the six prisoners from Allington. There is information I desire of them. Then check your guard. Have each post report. If any are found lacking, they are to be killed immediately. I will know how strangers came to aid the escape of the young woman. I will not have any rescue attempt succeed with the princes."

"It will be done," Brocahn assured.

Before long, the six princes stood before him, their faces grim. Aeol stiffened his shoulders. "What do you mean by bringing us to this place?"

Morgeth ignored his question. "There should be seven of you, yet one eludes my people. Where is your youngest brother?"

Lindulf opened his mouth, but Aeol silenced him

with a glance. "The last we saw Jeremian was the dinner to honor the queen."

"Who kept him from taking the draft?"

"The draft?" Duncan looked at Aeol. "Grilick's toast? He drugged the mead?"

"Silence," Aeol said as he shook his head. He faced Morgeth. "We do not know why Jeremian didn't drink, nor where he went."

"Who visited him? Did a girl named Estellyn show up for him that day?" Morgeth watched carefully. Duncan reacted. He stood in front of him. "You are familiar with her name?"

Duncan glanced at Snechtal.

Morgeth reached for Duncan, but Snechtal pushed him out of the way. "Only because I mentioned it to him."

"Snechtal, no," Aeol tried to quiet him, but Snechtal shook his head.

"I don't know why you need to know. She seemed of no importance. A villager Jeremian dabbled with."

"She is known to him." He looked at the warden. "I will not wait for the new moon. Prepare them for tonight. Inform Grilick of what is to be done." Morgeth gave the prisoners a bleak look before turning away.

"We've been betrayed," Olith swore as they were forced to return to their cold, dank cells.

"What do they mean to do?" Duncan struggled against the goblin holding his arms.

Aeol had no answers, there was only fear.

~

"This is not acceptable, Lord." Orlin shook with anger as a brute of a goblin nearly twice his size held him.

"Who were her companions?" Morgeth's eyes flashed.

"Companions? The two lads with her? They were her brothers."

His lip curled. "I don't think so. Was one of them Prince Jeremian?"

"Prince? Can't rightly say. I've never met a prince. But, yeah, Jeremian, I think that's a name she used. Didn't do her any good."

Lord Morgeth closed his eyes. "You had all three of them in your power, in your grasp."

"You asked for the girl. I brought you the girl. Unharmed, as requested, except for the bump on the head which couldn't be helped."

"Her friends were able to rescue her."

He shrugged. "Perhaps you need tighter security. It's a big world you have here."

"I will hold your life accountable for the three of them. Find them, or you will die."

Orlin opened his mouth to argue, then thought better of it. "No need for threats. We found them easily enough last time; this will prove no different."

"Send word when you have their location. My people will capture them."

Twenty-One

It was impossible to tell the passing of time. Aeol scowled at the food and a goblet of nasty-tasting liquid delivered without a word. None of his questions were answered. He couldn't hear his brothers, though he screamed through the grate of the door trying to connect with them. Sometime later, the door flung open, and a pair of goblins grabbed hold of him.

"Where are you taking me?" He pulled against them, but they were much stronger.

"Aeol!" Lindulf's voice was strained, fearful.

"Shut your mouth before we hit it." A goblin answered.

Snechtal's hands were tied behind him. In the dim light, Aeol could see blood on his face. Olith was there as well, being dragged along faster than he could get his feet under him.

They were led into an odd space. Aeol noticed a beach with water lapping against it. A bit of light gleamed on water near the shore. It seemed as though the water bobbed or was made to move by something beneath its surface. The stench of the place made him gag.

Further on the beach stood Morgeth. He was a tall, thin man with silver hair and pale skin. The dark gleam of his eyes made Aeol's skin crawl. As they drew closer, he noticed other details- the pointed ears, the terrible beauty of his face. Aeol stared. "You're an Elf."

He motioned for the goblin to pull Aeol closer. "I am Lord Morgeth, master of the Dark Realm. Soon to be master of Overworld as well."

Aeol shook his head. "The Dark Realm? It's a story, a myth out of ages past."

Morgeth took a step closer. "This is what happens when you forget the danger that lies beneath your feet. Your world has grown complacent. You fail to recognize the power roaming among you, and its meaning."

"What are you talking about?"

"At the first sign of the unicorn you should have known I would prepare to war against you."

"I don't understand, why have you brought us here?"

Goblins forced Duncan and Lindulf to fall on their knees in the water. Edmund, Olith, and Snechtal were set beside them. Aeol pulled against the goblin holding him. "What are you doing with them?"

Morgeth grabbed Aeol's hand. "You don't even know the power of your own blood." He drew a knife and cut across the palm of Aeol's hand.

He gasped in pain. His brothers cried out and struggled against their goblin captors. Aeol's blood dripped in the water. A faint hue of blue dissipated. Something in the water shifted, causing waves to rise before settling.

"What is in the water?" Olith gasped.

Morgeth stepped beside Aeol. "I need soldiers. I

was unable to capture the unicorn. Her sacrifice would have been much stronger. But one of your kind saved it from the trap. If war is to happen, I need a vast army." He glanced at the brothers staring at Aeol. "Your blood, and their blood, will make that possible." He raised his voice. "Cut off their heads. See it is done in the water."

Someone kicked the back of his leg, forcing him to fall on his knees. Duncan screamed and flailed. The others cried out as well.

"Brothers," Aeol closed his eyes and spoke with the authority of who he would have been. "We are sons of Aeoloch Fengormeth, of the house of Taighlais. By the Maker, if this is to be our end, we will face it with the honor of the good life we have led thus far."

"Where is Jeremian?" Edmund asked as a black-clad figure swung a long, thick sword. One moment, Edmund and Aeol had eye contact, the next, Edmund's body fell into the water. Aeol could not see where the head rolled. With each of them, he kept his gaze steady, though death gripped his heart. One by one, they fell. There was no rescue. No undoing. Tears poured down his face as he looked last upon Morgeth. "The Maker pay you for your deeds this day." he closed his eyes as the sword swung.

Twenty-Two

"He's feverish." Jeremian sat across from Estellyn, a low fire between them.

"We're so far west. Are there villages in the area? Someplace with a healer?"

Jeremian chuckled. "We are not beyond civilization. I think if we follow the road a bit further, we'll find an inn." He moved his head in the direction of Riven. "Get him a real bed and medicine."

She nodded. "Real food."

"If need be, I'll show my crest. Rooms for each of us. A good sleep and breakfast before we continue our way to Hoth."

Jeremian helped get Riven ready to walk, but Estellyn wasn't where he'd left her. The two men turned, staring through trees marking the edge of the farmland. "Estellyn," Jeremian hollered. His voice was swallowed up in the fields.

"They'll be looking for us. Have you no common sense?"

They both jumped and spun at the sound of Estellyn behind them. Jeremian gaped. "What is that?"

She led a scraggly horse. "He won't be much, but

Riven can ride. Save his energy. We'll move faster."

Jeremian took a step toward her, holding his hand up. "You can't steel a horse. It's a hanging offense."

Estellyn frowned. "I didn't steel it. I traded for it."

"Traded what?" He noticed she still held her walking stick.

"A prisoner in the Dark Realm… a dead one, he had a blue ring. I kept it. Seemed a good idea at the time. This proves I was right."

"A ring for a horse?"

She shrugged. "It had a big blue stone." She looked at Riven. "Think you can get on?"

"I've never ridden." His eyes glistened from the fever.

"It'll be easier than walking while you battle remnants of the spider poison."

"I'll help," Jeremian said, then gave the other man directions.

The sun had crossed into afternoon when they took the road from the farm in search of accommodation.

~

"Our friend is sick. We could use a pair of rooms, or three." Estellyn smiled at the red-headed young man assigning sleeping spaces. Jeremian had set Riven in a chair near the door and was moving toward her.

The young man squinted at a parchment on his desk. "I can do two rooms, across the hall from each other."

"We can work with that." She motioned for Jeremian to join her. "He," she looked at the young man, lifting a brow.

"Challon," he said with a grin.

She smiled back. "Challon is providing us with two

rooms. Upstairs and across the hall." She gazed at Challon. "Does one of them have a pair of beds?"

He nodded. "All our rooms do. Enough space for a third, if need be."

"I appreciate you can give us two. Is there a healer in this village? Our friend has a fever and I wanted to get him medicine."

"Aye. I'll send one of the barn lads for something." He handed her both keys. "Kitchen's still serving, if you wanted a meal before heading upstairs."

Jeremian thanked him. "We gladly accept an offer for dinner."

Challon faced Estellyn. "The lad'll find you in the common room. Ask for the honey ale. It's especially good this season."

Jeremian chuckled as he and Estellyn walked to Riven. "I think you have an admirer."

"Your identify has been kept secret, so I think that's good."

Riven opened his eyes when they drew near. "I feel I could sleep for days."

Estellyn offered her hand to help him stand. "A hot meal should help. They'll send someone to fetch medicine, as well."

He grimaced at the stairs. "Hopefully, I'll have the energy needed to climb to the rafters."

"We have rooms." Estellyn jingled the keys. "First floor. We can get you up a flight."

The common room had a scattering of tables and chairs in the main room and then a bar further on. No one paid them any heed as they chose an empty table near the fire.

They had drinks and were still waiting for the meal

when Estellyn stood. "I should take food to the horse."

"No," they both insisted.

Jeremian tugged her sleeve to get her to sit. "I already took care of the horse. I don't think any of us can handle a repeat of the other night just yet."

She slumped. "There is that."

"Are you waiting on an apothecary bag?" A boy stepped to the table.

"Yes," Estellyn said, grabbing the brown cloth bag sinched at the top.

Jeremian handed the lad a coin. "Thank you."

Riven eyed the bag warily. "What's in it?"

Estellyn unwrapped it and pulled out a vial with powder.

The boy nodded. "That's the one to mix with water. The other's a cake thing you can eat." He scrunched his nose. "Don't smell like cake."

Jeremian grinned. "Medicine never does." He pointed at one of the waiting ladies. "Could you fetch a glass of water for us?"

He trotted off as Estellyn handed Riven the biscuit-shaped cake. "At least you have some ale to wash it down."

He didn't seem to find the taste offensive. Once they had their meals, Estellyn noticed his color improving. "A good night sleep and early start tomorrow with fresh supplies."

Jeremian finished his drink and sank back with a sigh of contentment. "With the horse, we'll be able to carry better provisions."

Gathering supplies they would need could wait until morning. Estellyn sank onto the bed. The room was quiet. She opened the window shutter. The night noises were comforting. She fell asleep without hesitation.

Late in the night, a stabbing pain tore through Estellyn's side. She staggered from the bed, then fell, gasping for breath. Pain subsided and she almost pushed herself to her feet when the next wave struck. Her body slammed into a cabinet, causing it to thud against the wall. She grabbed hold of the cabinet door, trying not to fall again.

With a shout, Jeremian ran into the room, sword raised. He searched the room

Estellyn reached for him. "There are no others here." Her words ended on a cry.

Jeremian dropped his sword. The clatter didn't matter. He reached for her, sweeping her up in his arms.

She managed a few more breaths before pain stabbed again.

A roused taverness hovered in the doorway, holding a lamp. "What has happened?"

"We need a healer," Jeremian said as he laid her on the bed.

Estellyn didn't hear the reply. She curled, panting against the pain. "The staff. Bring me the staff."

Jeremian released her hand and disappeared. Pain muddled her thoughts. She latched onto the wood when he returned with it. Both hands gripped tight, and she rested her forehead against it.

The pain faded. She found herself in a wooded area filled with the silver light of stars shining far above. The air was cool yet moist, smelling like flowers mixed with pine. She looked down. Instead of the tunic and leggings she normally wore, a grown of green and azure floated around her. She held the staff in her hand. A bird sang from the trees. Others joined in. Their melody wrapped around her and drew her further into the woods.

Astebery quivered, the stallion behind her looked thick and impressive in stature. But at her side wobbled a slender foal, white as her parents yet touched with a star on her forehead. She was beautiful. A ridge of silky hair started at the crown of her head and flowed back. Her tail looked like silken threads. From her shoulders, feathered wings batted against the air for a moment then settled back at her sides. Her eyes sparkled green. Estellyn walked closer. Starlight lit her path. The stallion snorted, shaking his head. Gold sparkles flashed from his horn. He left them, disappearing in the woods.

Estellyn looked at Astebery with a puzzled frown. "What am I doing here?"

"Can't you tell?"

She swung around. Lystra stood nearby. "I experienced horrible pain."

"She doesn't understand pain. The feel of it must have sent her to you."

"She gave it to me so she wouldn't have to deal with it?"

"She's giving you more than that."

Estellyn turned back. Astebery held her gaze. She balked. "I'm not her mother. She needs a mother."

Lystra answered for Astebery. "You are her caretaker, as I have been for Astebery."

"I don't know how to care for a horse—unicorn," she corrected as a snort blew against the back of her head. "With wings. Have you ever seen a unicorn with wings?"

Lystra's face darkened. "A winged unicorn is rare, and not an omen for good to come."

"Not helping."

"You must protect her."

"I'm not even here, I don't think." She frowned. "I was in a bed at an inn." She swished the gown's skirt. "I own nothing like this."

The foal nipped at the fabric and Estellyn nuzzled her head. A strange emotion welled as she touched the unicorn, a fierce protective love. Joy, light, delight, excitement—a slew of emotions showered over her from the animal. "Hold on, Starlight." Estellyn held up her hand and the barrage of feelings simmered. Joy remained, causing her to laugh.

"You bond quickly."

"I don't understand. How can any creature hold so much joy for life within herself?"

"Your charge has no language, though she may understand yours when she wants."

"You are Astebery's caretaker?"

"Yes. This is her first child. She is pleased."

"Won't she miss her?"

"She brought life for a purpose, and she selected you to accompany that purpose. It is not our way, nor even the way of humans. The foal will experience mother's love through you."

"I don't know how to take care of her."

Lystra laughed. "This is no helpless baby. You will both survive."

Estellyn looked at the animal. Could she have grown taller while they'd been talking?

"You've named her?"

"Starlight." She ran her finger through the silver diamond shape on her forehead. "Yes, Starlight."

Starlight bounced closer.

Estellyn shook her head. "I work with cows, not

things with wings. Are you sure you want me? How will I find you?" Uncertainty faded away. Delight filled her. She wrapped arms around Starlight and bounced, giggling. The staff fell to the ground.

She woke in the bed at the inn. Jeremian held her hand while Riven stood close to the door.

"Don't move," Jeremian cautioned. "A healer is on his way."

Estellyn sat up, all signs of pain gone. "I'm alright, I'm not injured."

"But I saw you, you couldn't stand because of your pain."

"It wasn't my pain." She glanced at Riven. "Let them know we don't need a healer. Whatever it was passed quickly, and I am refreshed."

"Are you sure? At least have someone check you."

She grabbed his hand. "Truly, it was not my pain. Astebery has given birth to a unicorn." She peeked at the door, but no one was there. "A winged unicorn. I am to be her caretaker."

Jeremian shook his head. "Winged? That can't be possible."

Estellyn stood. "We must find her. She is the most beautiful creature you have ever seen."

~

Somewhere deep within the Dark Realm, a rock rolled and cracked.

Twenty-Three

From the crack in the stone spewed a pale flame followed by smoke and a squeak of surprise.

Julsi crouched behind a rock watching as the crack split further and something came through. A larger section of what she thought had been rock fell away. The creature inside stumbled and spilled onto the ground. Julsi checked the hall behind her. No one had noticed her slip away. She faced the creature. It was trying to push itself up, but its thin legs didn't seem strong enough to support itself. She glanced at her own scrawny legs and her foot with a slight twist. "They'll hurt you if they can. Nothing helpless is safe." With those thoughts in her mind, she limped to it and lifted it into her arms. Its body didn't seem warm enough, so she pressed it against her chest and wrapped her scruffy sweater over it. The creature hissed, then garbled. Julsi caressed its narrow head. "Don't be afraid, little one. I know where you can hide."

The wild eyes gentled, lids lowering. It nestled its head in the crook of her neck. Julsi made sure no one saw them. She clambered across the uneven ground. Sometime later, she slid into the cave. "I thought I was coming out here to die," she talked as she lit a small fire in an alcove. The cave twisted as it forged into the rock, so no light spilled out through the opening. She scrunched the blanket she used for sleep and laid the creature on it. "You're an ugly bird, hope you don't mind my saying. Still, you are safer here than out there on your own." She pulled the pack from her back. "I go to the work zone in the mornings. Foods not great, but it's not like anything grows down here." She frowned. "Except maybe you." The wedge of bread fell out first. It was hard to bite, but the taste was better than gruel. She tore a small piece and held it to the creature. Its nostrils twitched, but it didn't bother to eat.

Julsi sighed. "I should get the pieces from your shell. If someone were to find it, they may not like that you're down here." She tucked the blanket around the bird and scratched its chin. It gave a little chortle as though satisfied. Julsi dumped the contents of her bag. "I'll put the pieces in here and bring them back for you. Stay put, okay?" It curled and rested its head against its feet.

This time, Julsi took a short stick to help her walk better. Retracing her steps took time, but she found the broken shell. No one had disturbed it. She was opening the bag when she heard mumbling nearby. She lifted the pieces of shell into her bag. Each piece was about the size of her hand and heavier than she'd expected. She could barely stand without being pulled over and there were still two pieces remaining.

The voices were a way off. She searched the area then crawled across uneven ground where bits of rock jumbled. She wedged one piece of shell between the rocks then crawled further to hide the second piece. Her knees ached from the uneven rocks. She moved to the easier path, retracing her steps to find the stick.

Voices grew louder. Her heart stuck in her throat, but she needed the stick for walking.

"I'll find the unicorn. I'm not going to tell him otherwise."

"Better hurry. The goblins will grow stronger and faster with unicorn blood. If not that, he'll feed his useless servants—what's that?"

Julsi held her breath as she pressed her head into the rocks. Her body covered the stick.

"A rat, or maybe a dozen of them." The other one snarled. "You want to catch 'em? I'm sure they'll cook up nice."

There was a scuffle, the noise of which moved further away. Still, she waited.

"Come on," a gruff voice finally cursed. "I'm getting hungry. The slave's kitchen is closest."

Once again, the voices seemed to fade. After an exhaustible hour, Julsi lifted her head. She blinked but dark remained. She crawled backward taking the stick with her. Its pale wood seemed to give off a modicum of light.

When Julsi returned to the cave, the bird remained curled in the blanket. She set the stick against the wall where the cave turned into the mountain. In another little alcove, she dropped the stone-like remnants of the bird's shell. Something brushed against her arm, and she jumped, falling back on her bottom. The animal nuzzled her then sniffed at the shell. "I know you don't know better, but it's best not to sneak up on people." She tilted her head to get a better look at him. "It's amazing you fit in that thing at all. Unless you're already growing." She pulled herself to her feet and went to the back to rummage. "I've got a few bits of meat. Can you eat meat?" She took what she'd planned to eat and dangled it above. The long snout sniffed then bounced a little to get the morsel. With a laugh, Julsi released the treat before her fingers were nibbled.

The remaining portions provided entertainment for the evening. "Going to have to name you something. You resemble a red flame. Not the bad kind." She sighed. "I had a brother, not sure where he is now. His name was Cormac. Could I call you that?"

The creature settled rather than respond. Julsi shrugged. "Cormac will do."

~

Deep beneath the world, there was no change in light to mark morning. A rumble through the ground woke Julsi. Sleep tugged at her as she dressed for her shift in the mines. The fire had died to pale embers, and yet light flickered along the walls of the cave. She pressed her hands against her eyes as she yawned. There was still light. She glanced through the cave. The strange little bird had turned silver. Its chest moved as it breathed, and the light on the walls shimmered. She stepped on her twisted foot without thinking and fell to the ground with a cry. Cormac woke. Its head perked up then looked at her. He'd grown almost as big as she.

"I don't suppose Cormac will do," she scratched its head as it rested on her bent knee. "And you aren't really a bird, are you? Silverlight suits you better."

It stepped on her foot. There was an explosion of pain that caused her to gasp, but then it went away almost immediately. "What'd you do that for?"

It blinked, head still resting on her knee.

She narrowed her eyes. "I have to go work. I'll bring more food tonight. I know you probably don't understand me, but you're safer here. At least until I can find a way to get you up top." Julsi used the stick to help pull herself to her feet. She'd taken a few steps before she realized her foot was no longer twisted. She stared at the animal. "How did you… I dropped a rock and broke it years ago."

It blinked, then settled its head on its front legs and drifted to sleep. Julsi tapped her fingers against the walking stick, shook her head, and left the cave. She opened her little lantern enough to sneak along the path until she made her way to the bigger halls which led down into the mines. She dowsed the light and pressed her belongings into a small alcove where they wouldn't be noticed. She grabbed her tool bag.

She expected to see others ready for the long shift, but the paths were empty. Rumblings beneath her feet meant the next shift of miners should be underway, so how could there be no one stirring?

"We have slaves for this work." The sharp voice belonged to one of the henchmen.

Julsi scurried into a crevice.

"The dragon will come." A deeper gravelly voice barked. "The Dark Lord senses a hatchling is eminent. He must take control of the beast."

"A dragon?" The other scoffed.

"He will use it to destroy the unicorns once and for all."

Their voices faded. A dragon? Is that what she found? *Oh, Silverlight, you are in more danger than I.* Julsi retraced her steps. *No wonder sleep was hard to shake. It is too early.*

Her hands trembled by the time she returned to the cave. She stoked the glowing coals and added fuel to raise the fire. She turned and gasped. Silverlight had more than doubled in size, he bounced to his feet at the sight of her, making a chirping sound. She shook her head. "I have no new food for you, only the last of the bread. We must get out of here. If they find you, I fear they will do horrible things."

Mostly healed wounds on her back ached. Minions of the Dark Realm did not mind inflicting pain. He took the bread and nudged her. She shrugged. "Hopefully, we'll find more along the way."

Which way to go? She'd followed one trail and had seen blue sky far overhead. Too far overhead to be of any use to her. She chewed on her bottom lip. "But you have wings."

Decision made, she packed her few belongings in her bag and pulled it over her shoulders. She used tongs to remove one of the coals for the lantern then smothered the fire. She lifted the light and looked back at Silverlight. "I don't know if you understand me, but we have to get you out of here. Follow me." She paused to grab the stick, then paused again at the mouth of the cave. Nothing moved, no sound suggested others were watching. She went toward the labyrinth. When she glanced back, the dragon moved with her.

"They call this the labyrinth because the trails don't seem to lead anywhere." Having something to talk to encouraged her. "I found the body of a slave once. He left the main trail and got lost. I don't seem able to get lost. I can always find my way back." She paused then turned into a narrow tunnel. "Here, this way."

She crawled. The lantern knocked against a rock

and a spark burned her hand. She gasped. From behind, she heard Silverlight chirp. She sat and rubbed the spot. "It's okay. I've burned myself plenty of times. Or been burned." The dragon rubbed against her shoulder. "Come on, we're close." Soon the path opened to a huge space they could feel but not see. Julsi found a smooth rock to lean against. "I'm sure this is the place. It must be night. In the morning we should be able to see the way to get you out." She pulled her wrap from her bag and settled.

She slept, for when next she opened her eyes, far above was blue and daylight spilled through the opening to fall over the wave of rocks leading up to it. The blue dazzled, rich pure color after the world of gray. Silverlight stretched beside her. He lifted himself, peered at the opening, then looked back at her with a chirp.

"That is not a wall I can climb, but you can." She touched his wing. "Freedom is there for you; you must go away. Eldeneau is a village past the highland ridges and the moors beyond. Find refuge in the woods, away from any who would harm you."

He didn't seem inclined to move, so she crossed to the pile of rubble, crawling over the lowest rocks. He went with her. She sat when she could climb no more. "But you can."

He did. Step by step he found a way to cling and climb. Julsi made her way back down. She missed a footing and rolled. Grabbing a rock, she sliced her hand but stopped the plummet. Once she reached the bottom, she pressed her cut hand against her abdomen and looked up. Silverlight flapped his wings. Though she couldn't tell if he flew, he seemed to figure out how to use them to push forward. She watched his progress and as he stood against blue sky, she sobbed. The joy she felt for his freedom was tempered by her inability to follow. Her hand pained her as she walked back to her stuff. A shadow blotted out the light for a moment, causing Julsi to jerk around. "No!" Fear for Silverlight made her heart pound. Again, the shadow passed overhead, then something hurled through the opening. She caught a glimpse of huge wings and a long, lithe body. Another dragon had come. She clamored over the rocks back toward the tunnel, grabbing her stick.

An image of her leaning over with a morsel of bread blurted through her mind. Another of her sleeping and another of her far away, down at the bottom of the rocks looking up with hope. She stopped, hiding behind a boulder as she caught her breath. The images weren't hers. From across the cavern came the sound of chirps. Was it possible?

She peeked over the top of the boulder. It stood still, waiting.

"Silverlight? How?"

It slithered along the other side of where she stood. She saw herself climbing over and onto its back. "Why would I—" Then she looked up at the opening too far for her to reach on her own. Tears formed in her eyes. It was offering to take her. She didn't give herself time to think but crawled across the rock and onto Silverlight's back. She found footholds among the scales and stretched her arms wide as she could to hold on while burying her face. She felt him move. Fear made her dizzy, but she didn't loosen her grip. Her first sensation of freedom was the feel of sunlight on her back. Silverlight stopped. A moment later she released her hold. Leaning to one side she slid along the crevasse of his wing until she landed on the ground.

They were on a mountain, not inside of it. Trees grew nearby. Clouds dotted the sky. An unfettered breeze ruffled her hair. "You need to leave this place." Julsi wanted to bask in her unexpected freedom, but Silverlight remained. Still too close to danger. It moved closer, sniffing at her worn shirt. A thin tongue flicked against the blood. She pushed lightly. "That's my blood and I am not for eating." She grabbed the stick with her bloodied hand.

The openness of the space around them made her shake. Part of her wanted to go back, to be safe within the thick walls. But safety there was an illusion. She wiggled her foot. Something creaked in the mountain, and she hurried to Silverlight. Another image of her on his back came to mind. She shook her head. "I don't know where to go." The image remained and she finally returned to her place on his back. She kept her face pressed against his body as they left the mountainside.

Twenty-Four

"**What have you** done?" Grilick stood beside Morgeth staring at blood-stained sand and the bodies of men he'd known from birth. The water boiled and gurgled as a living thing.

"I need the seventh son. The power of their blood will not be at full strength without it."

Grilick blinked, swallowing the heavy knot in his throat. "You'll leave them like this?"

"What is said at the palace?"

"There are questions and concerns. The king and queen think it odd all their sons would leave without a farewell."

Morgeth smiled, a grim look that made Grilick regret choices he'd made. "I think it is integral to leave the House of Taighlais in no doubt of the fate of their sons." He waved a hand at the goblins standing gleefully nearby. "The bodies will be given to the water. Each son returns to his home. Let them have their final resting in their beds."

"Surely, that is more than necessary," Grilick protested.

Morgeth faced Grilick fully. "I want them to know

what has happened. Fear and sorrow will mar their hearts and prepare them for their own deaths. The goblins await you after night has fallen. Help them prepare my gift." He stepped closer. "Your own heart may quail, but do not doubt what will become of you if you fail me."

"No, my lord. I will do as you direct. There will be mourning through Overworld tomorrow."

"Come to me when it is finished so you may help locate Prince Jeremian. We do not want there should be hope that he survived."

~

Grilick stood on the balcony overlooking the valley as the sun rose. He closed his eyes. The housemaids would be lighting fires in the kitchen and dining room before heading to the sleeping quarters to clean up from the previous night and have a fresh fire going as the royal family awoke. Even if they thought the princes were away, they would prepare their rooms, just in case.

The sun had not inched far above the horizon when the first screams could be heard. Six of the princely suites had a gristly head propped on a pillow in the middle of their bed. Nothing would indicate who murdered them. No reason would be given.

Grilick closed his eyes. Someone had seen him go into the cellar. His part could not be hid for long. He gripped the railing, breathed, and opened his eyes to stare at the sun. The thought of redemption came to mind. Go to King Aeoloch and reveal the plot of Lord Morgeth. Perhaps there was a way to save Allington. Almost, he released the railing, but the part of him still loyal to King Aeoloch and the House of Taighlais had grown too weak. Lord Morgeth would find him and torment his failure to bring Jeremian. Torment with death long in coming.

Grilick gritted his teeth. He didn't look down, just pushed himself off the balcony. Darkness consumed him as he fell to his death.

Twenty-Five

Julsi's body ached from the effort of clinging to Silverlight. Trees surrounded a small field shielding the area where they finally landed. Julsi slid to the ground and lay in grass beneath the waning afternoon. "You must be starving. Can you eat grass?" She sighed when the animal set to grazing. "I wish I could eat grass." She forced herself to get up and walk along the edge of the woods. Mushrooms and purple fruits grew in the spaces between trees. She popped a fruit into her mouth and the taste was almost more than she could bare. She fell to the ground, eyes swimming with tears. "Whatever you do, don't wake up," she muttered as a barrage of emotion swept over her.

Then Silverlight joined her. He curled around and rested his head beside her. "I don't understand why I'm crying. Freedom is what I've hoped and dreamt for. But look at me, I'm shaking." She held up her hand. An image of a little girl came to mind. "Yes, I was taken. Our village was taken. I was with my brother, but we got separated. I haven't seen any of them since." She leaned against him. "Do you have memory of family?"

The image he impressed was being held in her

arms. Her body relaxed and fear dissipated. "I like that." She fell asleep.

Hours had passed when she woke. Silverlight kept her warm. There were no noises. Night surrounded them, but not like the deep blackness she'd grown accustomed to in the Dark Realm. The sky above them lit with a thousand points of light. There were no clouds or moon, just stars glittering with abandon. She lay and looked as long as she could, and even her dreams became filled with them.

Excitement woke her as the sun lifted above the hills in the east. The edges of rock glowed, then colors spread into the air. The sun rose with its orange hue. Trees formed long shadows. Julsi wrapped her arms around her legs as she hugged her knees. She'd seen such a sight, long ago, its memory nearly faded. Her grumbling stomach pulled her from staring.

She foraged for more to eat. "Hopefully, we can find a village today. Get some real food." She tilted her head. "But what of you? You can't go into a village. I'm not sure you would be safe." She thought a few minutes as she popped more berries into her mouth. "We'll have to look for an abandoned farm near a village."

Getting on the back of the dragon seemed natural. Its body length was about twice her own. "Can't really tell how long the wings are," she thought as she squeezed her eyes shut. Images of the ground below them appeared in her mind. "Not helping," she muttered. "Wait, the road. Follow the road."

A village appeared swiftly, causing Julsi to open her eyes. Thatched roofs. Houses built on top of each other. People walking freely. "Stay out of their sight," she warned.

They landed in a field. The large gray barn leaned precariously, but the rafters held remnants of winter hay. Silverlight stretched across weathered wooden planks on the ground and dug into the hay. Julsi rolled her eyes then went in search of food more appealing to herself.

Her growling stomach couldn't keep the impression of rustling leaves from bringing tears to her eyes. The twittering chirp of a cardinal stopped her altogether. So long bereft from the delights of nature, her mind wanted to savor every moment. Her stomach drove her on. The path led down a hill and across another. When she reached the peak of the next one, the village spread before her. The sight of houses crowded together was not as tangled from the ground as it had been in the sky. Noise assaulted her, but it wasn't what she expected. Voices lamented. Wafts of burning sage and myrrh drifted with the slight wind. The people she saw dressed for mourning in black tunics and caps covering their hair. Julsi stopped a woman carrying a bottle of oil. "What has happened?"

"You aren't from here."

The hard stare make Julsi want to slink away. She cleared her throat. "I was a slave forced to work in mines beneath the mountains. I don't know where I am from. I was too small when I was taken to remember."

The look gentled. "You poor dear. The world is a harsh place and peace cannot come swift enough to save us. Word reached us from the council of Hoth. The princes of Allington have been killed."

"All of them? Were there many?"

"Seven."

The growl of her stomach precluded any response. Julsi hung her head.

The woman sighed. "I don't have much, but you are welcome to share."

Julsi knew she should hesitate, but she didn't want to. What the mistress called simple and limited was more than Julsi saw in a week. She broke a wedge of bread and dipped it in the creamy stew. When the other woman ate, Julsi bit into the wet bread. Flavor burst in her mouth, making her cough and choke. She spluttered and looked down, cheeks growing hot.

"It has been a long while since you've eaten." The woman's voice remained calm. "Try small bites, like this."

Metal twanged against metal as the woman tapped her spoon against the edge of the bowl. Julsi watched, them mimicked what she saw. The flavor brought tears to her eyes, but she didn't spit it out again. When she was no longer hungry, she noticed the shadows had changed beyond the windows. "I need to go."

"Stay here. Help me with some afternoon chores. I can offer you a room to sleep. More food in the morning. I can make it plain, perhaps that would suit you better for a while."

Julsi stood, shaking her head. "I cannot stay, but I thank you for your kindness." Before the woman could decide to restrain her, Julsi slipped away. Her stomach rumbled some as she cut between houses, then saw a way through to the fields beyond the village. The sun had not moved much when she returned to the barn.

A screech alerted her to trouble.

Twenty-Six

Jeremian watched Estellyn as they walked from the inn toward the barn. Her pain had been real, and yet, she was fine. From her quick steps, he thought she seemed excited even.

"She won't be there," Estellyn told them again as they reached the open doors.

Jeremian shook his head at the empty barn. "Then where is she? How did you see her last night?"

"The glen in the highlands." She seemed certain.

"What glen?" Riven looked at them.

"It's a magic place. I cannot tell more than that."

"Because she doesn't know any more than that," Jeremian added as he glanced from Riven to Estellyn. "It will take most of the day to get there."

"Still," Estellyn pulled her pack on before donning her cape, "we are closer than if we'd been at Allington or my farmhouse."

They left before sunrise, following the main road. It was late afternoon when Estellyn led them into an overgrown hillside.

~

"This isn't even a real trail," Riven muttered as he

clawed his way up the incline.

"Just a little further," she said, offering her hand.

He accepted. The slight tug helped him pass a sharp outcropping of rock. Her touch swept tiredness from him. He continued without further assistance.

"We're here."

The impossible climb ended at a flat green field dotted with trees with gray mountains far beyond them. Riven sat, unmindful of the others hovering over him. He closed his eyes for a moment. The air seemed sweeter, fresher than the valley. The grasses beneath his fingers tickled with their softness. A laugh formed inside him at the thought of rolling across the clearing. He glanced up and froze. At first, he thought two horses, one smaller than the other, played in the distance. They seemed to be prancing and chasing. There was something about them, though. Something more than he ever imagined possible. Though he didn't understand why, the sight of them stole his breath. He sat, awed, staring.

The young animal jumped when it noticed Estellyn, then galloped across the field to her. Estellyn laughed as the two of them fell together, rolling in the field. This close, he saw the horn. "A unicorn." Nothing prepared him for a vision of pure goodness.

"You must wash in the well."

He jumped as a strange woman spoke. She was tall, with the same pointed ears as Morgeth. He scurried away from her.

She smiled, holding up her hand. "I am not one to fear. The mare wants you to bathe. There is something for you."

Jeremian turned. "He's with us."

Lystra smiled. "Yet still, he should wash in the

well."

Riven stumbled getting to his feet. "Where is it?"

"Follow the stream and you will find a circle of rocks. That is the well. We will wait here for you."

He entered the glen alone. Birds chatted in the trees. The stream gurgled and rushed, and then he saw the circle of stone surrounding what he would call a pool. Beyond it, the stream continued its path.

He pulled off his boots, sat on the rocks, and dipped his legs in the water. He'd expected cold mountain water, but this was warm. After laying his clothes on the rocks, he plunged in.

He was a boy, three or four years old.

"Gaiden," a woman called to him, taking him by the hands and bouncing him up and down in the water so he could splash. She sang to him as they played.

Riven shook his head, returning to himself, and moved to the edge of the pool, hands against the rocks. "What is this?"

The woman tilted her head and looked at him. "This is your memory."

He shook his head. "I was created by the dark lord, Estellyn transformed me."

Her brown eyes gleamed with tears. "No, you are my son. You were born free then taken when the dark one destroyed our village." Tears dripped on her cheeks. "I did not know you lived."

"Are you alive?" The truth of what she said unlocked something within him.

"No." Her smile defied any sorrow he might feel. "The Maker provided us this moment."

He felt tightness grip his throat from within. "Are there more memories?"

She smiled. "You don't need them. Who you are now will give you good memories to blot your years of service to the dark lord. You are not his." She faded and he stood alone in the pool.

"I don't understand." He glanced around but there was no one else in the glen. The memory of playing in the water with his mother remained.

~

"Where will you go now?" Lystra asked as they waited for Riven to return.

Estellyn looked at Jeremian. "I think we need to go to Hoff. The seer of Allington said I would meet the seer of Hoff and he might tell us more."

Lystra considered her direction. "Forces are building. Not even I understand. Morgeth moves to attack Overworld."

Jeremian paced nearby. "You think a dragon has already hatched?"

Lystra nodded. "It happened at the same time Starlight was born."

Estellyn gasped. "When I touched his arm, I saw a vision of a dragon attacking her."

Lystra frowned. "You touched Morgeth? Why would you dare such a thing?"

Estellyn felt her ears turn red. "The change it made in Riven."

Lystra shook her head. "Morgeth is nothing like Riven. You saw a vision, but what did he take from you?"

"I don't know. He tried to kill me right after."

"The spiders would not kill; they would turn you into an evil servant." Her eyes narrowed. "He would only do that if he thought you had power."

Riven's return stopped the conversation. Estellyn tightened her fist on her walking stick. Power seemed to come from the stick, but she didn't have it with her in the Dark Realm. Her focus turned to Riven. At first, with her mind preoccupied, she didn't notice any difference. But when she could see his eyes, the word that came to mind was hope. She glanced at Lystra. The Elf woman didn't seem to take any notice of Riven, and she didn't want her to try to force him to explain. She would ask him about it later.

Astebery and Starlight moved closer.

"Ah," Jeremian broke the tension with a grin. "You bathe and everybody's satisfied."

~

Morning brought a strange sight. "This cannot be Starlight," Jeremian gasped at the fully-grown winged unicorn.

Estellyn rubbed Starlight's mane as she wondered at the transformation. "She's coming with us. Astebery remains here."

"Where are we going?" Riven asked.

Estellyn looked at Jeremian who nodded. "We head to the village of Hoff."

Starlight might look like a grown beast, but her playful nature kept them entertained. She pulled apples from a high branch, causing water to splash over Jeremian. He yelled and Estellyn laughed. At one point, Starlight bopped Riven to help him over a rock. He bopped her back, then found out her wings had power.

"Starlight," Estellyn called when she chased after a butterfly. Estellyn waited with her hands on her hips. When Starlight returned, the black and gold butterfly sat on the tip of her horn. 'Yes, it's very pretty," she told the unicorn. "Now, have it fly away. I don't think your wings work the same as hers. When we get to a large enough field, watch some birds and give it a try."

That Starlight understood Estellyn became obvious, when, at the edge of a meadow, Starlight stood beneath a tree staring up at a sizeable bird with red wings and black body. She neighed, and the bird hopped along.

"We're stopping for flying lessons?" Jeremian said as he stood beside Riven. They watched as Silverlight bounded across the field, practicing moving her large wings. The black bird moved along with her.

Riven frowned. "Can a bird teach a different beast how to fly?"

"Starlight's language is something all living things recognize," Estellyn shrugged.

As they settled for the night, Starlight lived up to her name, seeming to gleam in the dark with the same pale light as the stars above. Estellyn sat beside Riven while Jeremian searched for wood to build a fire. She tilted her head as she watched him. "What happened at the well?"

Riven took a deep breath. "I have a memory."

"From where?"

He laughed. "Playing in the water with my mother when I was a young boy." He shook his head.

Estellyn gripped her hands in her lap to keep from touching him. "You were a goblin."

"But was I created that way, or cursed by the dark lord?"

Estellyn had no answer, nor did she want one. What if the goblins were ordinary people stolen and twisted into something horrible? She closed her mind against thinking about them. "I brought enough vegetables from the village to make soup." She rose, then looked at Riven. "I am glad you have a memory that proves you are not what you thought." She went to prepare their meal as Jeremian returned to start the fire.

Late in the evening, as everyone lay quiet, dark thoughts played through her mind. She shifted, facing Starlight. The unicorn nudged closer until Estellyn could scratch between her ears. Starlight touched Estellyn's forehead with her horn. The darkness seemed to strip back and the stars above them blazed. The beauty of it drove away her dark thoughts. She stared, caught up in the dreams of a unicorn.

The peace and beauty of those moments stayed with her as they journeyed the following day.

Jeremian paused. "We're getting close enough to the village we should find a place to stay for the night. There are plenty of abandoned farms in this area."

"Are we close to Hoff?" Estellyn looked around.

"We're still a few days, but we won't find the open places to spend the night like we have."

Starlight pranced and shook her head. Estellyn placed a hand on her neck. "Something disturbs her."

They looked but noticed nothing. Riven pointed. "There's an old structure ahead. Perhaps something is waiting inside."

They drew closer but still didn't see anything. Jeremian noticed a well with a rope wrapped around a pulley. He tugged and felt something. "There's a bucket. Let's hope this well still has water."

It did, and they found a trough so Starlight could drink. She still seemed nervous about something. The three of them went around the other side to check the barn. Jeremian grabbed hold of Estellyn's arm.

"Something is inside." He spoke in a low quiet voice.

Estellyn stopped. He was right. Something large lurked in the shadow within.

There was a chirp, then a thud they could feel through their feet. What came into view made them all gasp. The thing jerked its head up. Estellyn would have said it was as surprised by them as they were by it. Then, with a screech that made her want to cover her ears, it bounded away. Around the side of the barn. Toward Starlight.

Twenty-Seven

Julsi thought she saw people moving through the trees. "Don't hurt him," she ran screaming through the trees. Dragon cry caused the branches to shudder. Ahead, in a clearing, she could just make out Silverlight's tail twitching. She veered her course.

The dragon crouched with a hissing sound shooting sparks into the air. The white horse reared, front legs slashing. "He's not going to hurt you," she screamed again, racing to put herself between the two of them. Silver glinted in the hooves of the horse. Julsi covered her face and cowered but didn't move. She felt the earth vibrate as the powerful legs struck the ground. Something pushed against her back. Silverlight snorted behind her.

Julsi peeked through her fingers. The horse with a great horn pointing to heaven shook its mane, causing her to squeak.

"Are you mad? Get away from there." A strange woman yelled as she ran toward them.

"He'll kill you." Someone else shouted.

"No, he won't. He's not like that," Julsi crossed her arms, keeping an uneasy eye on the strange horse.

"I'm not sure what you think you know," the man said as he held his hands with palms facing her and taking small steps in her direction. The dragon's tail flickered, and he paused. "Dragon's nature is not to be harmless."

The horse shook again and backed up a few steps. Julsi watched. "His nature is forged, as is ours." She noticed a second man with dark hair and pale skin who had a way about him that made her want to run. "You're not like the others."

"I lived in the Dark Realm a very long time."

"The unicorn and the dragon seem a lot less anxious than you." The woman motioned in the direction of the animals. "Night will be here soon enough, and I prefer having shelter nearby. How about we call a truce and get settled. We can share stories over a fire."

The dragon curled up outside beside the chimney with its head close enough to the door it could listen. Julsi frowned at it. The horse—unicorn as the others called it—had a stall inside.

"Who are you?" The woman asked as she motioned to a pillow on the floor for a seat.

"I'm Julsi. I was captured and taken to the Dark Realm as a child." She glared at the dark man.

The woman nodded. "I was there as a prisoner not so long ago."

Julsi jumped to her feet. "You lie. If you were a prisoner, you would still be there."

"She had help in her escape." The dark man spoke. "I am Riven. I was servant to the master of dark. Whether by lifting of a curse, or some other means, I was changed by Estellyn."

"Estellyn?"

The woman nodded. "I grew up on a farm. I wouldn't be in this mess if it wasn't for Starlight's mother."

"Starlight? Is that the unicorn's name?"

A soft bray sounded from the shadows. It was answered by a snort near the doorway. Julsi giggled. "He is Silverlight."

Estellyn leaned forward. "In all the tales, dragons are evil. How can he be different?"

"I found him breaking out of his shell. I hid him from the goblins and led him to where he could go free. He returned and brought me out as well. Does that sound evil to you?"

"No." She furrowed her brows. "I don't understand."

"I overheard them speaking, if they found him, they would break him. They would use him to hunt the unicorns and destroy them."

"What if that's what he decides to do?"

"Your horse tried to kill me, too. Does that make her good?"

"She's a unicorn, a very special unicorn who can fly."

"Silverlight is special, too."

A taller man entered the barn shelter. "Suffice to say they are both special." He was taller than Riven, with light hair and wide shoulders.

"This is Jeremian," Estellyn introduced.

"Prince Jeremian?" Her voice quieted as memories tried to surface, memories of screams and pain.

"The youngest son. The title really doesn't matter."

Estellyn watched Julsi. "You know him?"

Julsi shook her head. "I must have known of him

long ago."

Riven paced closer. "You overheard talk about using the dragon to destroy unicorns?"

She nodded.

"Did you hear why?"

"That's all I remember hearing. I was trying to hide from them."

Jeremian fidgeted with his pipe. "My part in this started because of the Seer. What if we pay him a visit? Maybe he can see what is happening, why all these parts are coming together."

Julsi stood. "There is something else. I visited the village today."

"It isn't one I'm familiar with." Jeremian glanced from her to Estellyn. "You?"

Estellyn shook her head.

"It was a somber place, most everyone dressed in black." She looked at Jeremian. "The Council at Hoth sent word that the seven princes had been killed."

Jeremian stiffened. "You lie."

"Why would you think that? I don't know any of you, why would I have reason to lie?"

Estellyn moved closer to Julsi. "He is who he claims to be. I've seen him practicing swords in the weapons yard at the castle. If they're wrong about one, maybe their wrong about the others." She looked at Jeremian. "Another reason to go to Hoth."

"Hoth is still a three-day journey. How do we do that with a dragon?" Jeremian asked.

"Why would it go with us?" Riven glanced at the long tail twitching outside the open barn side.

Julsi blinked. "The enemy will be after him."

"And when it decides to eat us?" Jeremian argued.

Julsi glared. "He eats grains."

"Until he gets a taste of meat."

She crossed her arms and straightened. "What do you know? There hasn't been a live dragon for hundreds of years."

"But in all the stories, dragons are evil."

She stiffened her shoulders. "They were used for evil. Silverlight won't be."

Estellyn broke in. "Argue all you like, but I think we should stay together. We may need each other."

Jeremian huffed and walked away. Julsi watched a moment then turned to Estellyn. "What does he have to do with any of this?"

"They want to kill him. He needs protecting."

"Does your unicorn fly?"

"She's not my unicorn," Estellyn laughed. "We're companions. And yes, she flies."

"What if we use the unicorn and dragon to get to Hoth? We'd travel faster, wouldn't we?"

"I don't know. I've never been that far myself. Jeremian," Estellyn called him over when he turned. "Do you think we could get to Hoth faster by flying on the unicorn and dragon?"

"Fly? We can't do that."

"Estellyn says Starlight can carry her. I know Silverlight carried me and he's already a bit thicker so I think he could handle two of us."

"And Riven?" Jeremian asked as the other man joined them.

"What about me?"

Estellyn considered a moment. "He should be with me. A lighter load for Starlight."

"Lighter load?" Riven's eyebrows lifted. "You

want me… that unicorn is not going to let me on her back."

"She may for necessity's sake."

"Doesn't matter. A unicorn is a Holy creature. I am of the Dark Realm."

Estellyn laid her hand on his arm. "You have been redeemed."

Jeremian cleared his throat. "I'm more concerned with the dragon than the unicorn."

Julsi huffed, then stood and reached her hand toward Jeremian. "Come on."

"Where?"

"Time for you to get over your predilection to think ill of Silverlight." She grabbed his hand and pulled him to the open side of the barn, ignoring his protests.

Moving around the tail, they stood by the body of the dragon who rested a bit like a cat in a sunny window. Jeremian hesitated as Julsi tugged to get him closer. She finally huffed, hands fisted on her hips. "How many dragons have you met?"

He frowned. "Well, none, of course."

"Actually, you've met one. Has he done anything to make you think he's dangerous?"

Silverlight lifted his head. Jeremian swallowed. "No, he hasn't."

"Then come on." She took his hand again and turned. She placed her other hand on the dragon's neck. Its smooth scales were warm and moved slightly as he breathed. Jeremian placed his hand beside hers.

Julsi thought about flying, the two of them on Silverlight's back. The next image carried with it the sensation of soaring. Then it changed to a dark cave with flickering flames of red. They both jerked their hands from the dragon. Jeremian tightened his jaw. "That is what we must face."

She shuddered. "You saw that?"

He nodded. "It must be the Dark Realm, but where?"

"Those were goblin pools."

"You know of those things?"

"Very little, thank the Maker. Those who go to it, never return."

Jeremian looked at the dragon with a glint of respect in his eyes. "Could you find them?"

"I could. Why?"

"They say the pools are breading grounds for an army. When their numbers are great enough, they will attack the surface world." He peeked at Silverlight. "Dragons are capable of destroying entire cities. Could he burn the pools?"

"I don't know that he's made fire. How do we know fire isn't just part of a myth?"

Jeremian placed his hand on the dragon again. "The only purpose I've known for dragons is to hunt and harm. Yet here is one contrary to that." He looked at Julsi. "We need to visit the Seer."

LAURIE LEE

Twenty-Eight

"I think this is the closest to Hoff we dare get with a dragon," Jeremian jumped to the ground. Julsi followed him. Starlight drew in her wings and landed in a field. Estellyn and Riven managed to keep their seat until she stopped. Jeremian hid a grin. Riven seemed a bit green as they joined them in a back field of an abandoned farm.

"Should we all go into Hoff?" Julsi askes as she and Riven watched the others prepare a fire and forage for food.

"If what they're saying about the princes is true," Estellyn looked at Jeremian, "it may be best to keep you a secret."

"But I have to go. I have to know." He glanced at Riven. "Whose fault is it if they are dead?"

"Won't the seer see through a disguise?" Julsi leaned forward as small flames licked the wood.

"The seer won't be a problem."

"I think we should all go," Riven spoke without lifting his head. "Whatever happens, or what needs to happen, involves us all."

"Leave Starlight and Silverlight? Is that safe?"

"Starlight is just a baby," Estellyn protested.

"So is the dragon. They were born on the same day." Julsi crossed her arms. "They get along better than some of the humans I've met." She blushed. "I mean, met in the Dark Realm, not you."

Jeremian tossed a small log on the growing fire. "Riven is right. We all need to speak with the seer. But not today. I say we sleep here. There should be shelter in that abandoned barn." He peered at each of them in turn, then nodded at their silent agreement.

After a warm meal around the fire, they explored the dwindling structure. There wasn't much that hadn't already been looted by locals, but it was dry and had a fair amount of decent hay to pack under the sleeping mats.

Though morning started gray with a fine mist in the air, their plans didn't change. Hoff was somber in its mourning. The four of them walked through the gates without pause. A few farmers brought necessities, but no other travelers were on the road. Jeremian slumped his shoulders and kept the hood of his travel cape drawn over his head, hiding his face from the few curious onlookers. Julsi had no cloak or cape. She wrapped herself in a wool blanket to ward off the chill as they walked. Estellyn and Riven both had something. Jeremian led them from the main street. The twists and turns did not phase Julsi, but the seer was something different.

She stared at the old man sitting on a bench outside a small house. None she knew ever survived within the Dark Realm. She didn't know the gray of his eyes meant he was blind.

"There is much within you, Child."

He must be talking to one of the others, but he's looking straight at me. She peeked at the others. His focus did not linger on her, and she was glad when he greeted them.

"We should go inside." He stood suddenly. "Help an old man, my boy." He stretched his arm, seeming to feel around for something. Jeremian jumped forward, letting him take his arm.

Julsi frowned as she moved closer to Estellyn. "Is he blind? How can a seer be blind?"

"I don't think his sight is for what's around him."

The main room of the house had posts about a foot from each corner and beams crossing the ceiling. The open door and windows made the space bright. There were stools and benches, wicker rockers and fauteuil, a low foot stool and high back chairs. More lined the walls. The seer had Jeremian guide him to a stuffed chair with worn arms. "It does my heart good to know you yet live, my prince." He motioned at the supply of seats. "Choose what suits you. This is a room for meetings."

"What of my brothers? Why did you not warn me they were all in danger?"

"There is an order to things, my prince. Choose your seat and introduce me to your company. The past will not change in these few moments."

"He's right," Estellyn touched his arm.

Jeremian drew back his hood with a sigh. The others were already sitting. Estellyn sat beside a high back chair she'd pulled closer for him. Riven sat on a stool a little further back than the other three. Julsi used a short foot stool and had her legs crisscrossed on the floor. Jeremian unhooked his travel cape, draping it on the back of the chair. "Thank you." He motioned at Estellyn. "Estellyn is a farmer's daughter from the highlands."

The seer laughed. "She is many things, but a farmer's daughter is not one of them. What of the other two? They've spent time in the Dark Realm."

"Julsi and Riven. Their stories are theirs to tell if they choose."

The seer faced Jeremian with a sightless stare. All remained quiet for a few moments. "You are wise and foolhardy. To allow them their own telling is a kingly gesture."

"I am not supposed to be king." Jeremian remained standing beside his chair.

"That is not for you to decide."

"What happened to my brothers? I went looking for the unicorn to save Edmund, but now all of them are dead?" His voice broke.

"Your search and what you found saved your life. There was nothing you could have done except die with them."

"Why didn't you let me know? They could have been hidden away."

"Only the Maker has perfect sight. I knew of one brother's peril."

"Was it his fault?" Jeremian pointed at Riven.

Surprisingly, the seer faced Riven. "Ah, you are not what you think."

"I am a servant of the Dark Lord."

"You were a slave, twisted to his design, but he could not have given you human form if you did not already possess it."

"Do you mean the memory at the well is real?" Riven's voice held both disbelief and hope.

"You are a child of the world, taken in your youth long before the young woman." He turned to Julsi. "I am sorry for the loss of your family. Lord Morgeth did not know what he had in you, or you would have been destroyed long ago."

"Me?" Julsi squeaked.

The seer smiled. "Only you could have turned a dragon from its being."

"You know about the dragon?" Jeremian finally sat.

"And the unicorn. They are all tied together. It is the reason your brothers died."

"But no one knows about the unicorns."

"The Dark Lord knew." Estellyn started to put the pieces together. "He trapped the mare, planning to sacrifice her before she could birth a foal. Since I helped her escape, she's alluded him, and the stallion found her. Once Morgeth knew a foal would be birthed, he's been planning war with Overworld."

The seer nodded. "A new foal means a new dragon. But a dragon is not enough to win a war. He needs soldiers. Many of them. Though I cannot see inside the Dark Realm, I know there are deep brooding pools. Your royal blood feeds his monsters, pits them against your people. The death of six princes means he's making no small army."

Julsi shook. "How could he know?"

He furrowed his thick brows, "Dark and light are in constant battle. They will always know what best upsets the balance."

"What do we do? How do we fight against the Dark Realm army?"

"You don't." Riven shook his head. "To fight is folly."

"We will not give up without a fight." Estellyn

spoke with a grim tone. "How long does it take for his army to grow?"

"He only needs a few weeks. You have mere days before the war will begin."

"We have no army to face such an enemy." Jeremian rubbed his eyes.

"Our only hope is to destroy his army before they emerge."

"Impossible."

"You have a dragon." The seer interjected. "This young lady can get him in undetected."

"Then what?" Riven looked at Julsi. "None but the foulest know how to find the pools. Even at my worst, I never went there."

Julsi chewed her bottom lip. The seer was looking at her. Well somehow looking without looking. "I can find them. I don't get lost, not even in the labyrinth."

The seer closed his eyes. "If he knows of the dragon, the Dark Lord will put all his thought to bending it to his will." He opened his eyes and stared in Julsi's direction. "Not even your powers can protect the beast against him forever,"

"Then we need to distract him." Estellyn glanced from Jeremian to Riven.

Riven shook his head. "He captured you once, and you escaped. Don't expect such good luck a second time."

"What other way is there? Silverlight needs to be able to go deep into the Dark Realm without hinderance."

"If you simply go into his realm, the Dark Lord will know you have come with a purpose You must allow yourselves to be captured. I have a good idea where this can take place." The seer nodded.

"Julsi shouldn't be alone." Estellyn shifted in her seat. "Riven goes with me and Jeremian stays with Julsi and the dragon."

"No," Jeremian protested.

"If we let you be captured, they may try to kill you before the others can get in place. He'll want to toy with me like he did before, but you he'll kill straight up if it benefits the army."

The seer sighed. "I cannot tell you if there is wisdom in your plans or if you go to death in vain."

"Let us live with hope," Julsi stood. "We have more than people will have if we do nothing."

The time with the seer ended. All were quiet as they walked through the cool spring afternoon. Though the village remained still, signs of life and hope after winter could be seen in the spaces turning green. As they returned to the old farmhouse, Starlight rode out to greet them. Estellyn smiled at the bits of grass and leaves caught up in the young horse's coat. "At least you've been having some fun."

It appeared Silverlight had as well. A burnt tree tilted close to the earth. The dragon lay beside it, head raised and tail twitching, as though eager to display his prowess. Julsi found a spot near his ear hole where he particularly enjoyed a good scratch. He flopped to his side to give her a better reach.

Jeremian stood looking up at the tree. "At least we know he can make fire."

Estellyn looked at Riven. "We need to go. It will take a few hours to get to the other village riding the unicorn."

The four of them stood close for a moment.

Jeremian smiled. "We are an odd company. By the Maker, I hope we are able to meet like this again."
"By the Maker," the rest of them repeated.

Twenty-Nine

The village of Runce was not known for a gentile population. Its outer walls were made of iron and wood. Estellyn stood in the shadow of a barn looking down at dull colors spread across rickety shelters. Even from a distance, a stale odor wafted in the breeze. Dark places with lots of shadows could be seen in the afternoon light. "I get the feeling people don't want their deeds to be known."

Riven moved to stand beside her. "You don't belong here."

"It's the best chance I have to get taken." She walked to Starlight, stroking the nose of the unicorn. "You'll follow, won't you? But be careful. Don't want you to get captured."

Starlight's shake of her head indicated she understood.

Riven sighed. "We need to go."

Estellyn used her cloak to keep herself from view as they entered Runce. Several others peered at her, but the glare of Riven soon sent them on their way. He arranged lodging for the night, though she doubted they would need it for long.

~

"I'm not so sure of this plan," Riven stood in the doorway of a strange room in the strange village of Runce, far from anything he knew.

"The seer seemed to think workers of the Dark Realm will be here." She shivered. "I think he is right."

"I did not have to go into the presence of the Dark Lord when we rescued you. It will not take much to turn my will to his."

"Let us hope you go unnoticed." Light from the setting sun spilled into the room. "Come here."

Riven joined her at the window. She lifted her hand so light splashed across her skin. "Put your hand next to mine." He did. "What do you feel?"

"Warmth."

"Soak it into your mind so even in the dark beneath the earth you can remember. Hold to that light."

He joined his hand to her. "What if I hold to you?"

Rather than answer, she rested her head against his shoulder and allowed him to wrap an arm around her. They stood in the window, watching the sun set and shadows spread. When the shadows began to move, she straightened. "It is time."

~

Jeremian walked beside the dark-skinned girl as they gave the dragon a rest from carrying them both. Rather than pay attention to the beast on their heels, he studied her. She was younger. The color of her eyes seemed to shift from blues to greens. "You're so small," he suddenly blurted. "How did you survive as a slave in the mines?"

She answered after a moment of silence. "No one really noticed me, not even after I broke my foot and limped."

He looked down. "You walk fine now."

"Silverlight healed me. Before that, I used a stick to help me walk. Other slaves expected it to break, but it never did." She tilted her head as though listening to something he couldn't hear. "Silverlight is ready to fly again." She rubbed her arms.

Jeremian placed a hand on her shoulder. "Courage."

She nodded. "We'll both need it."

~

"This is not a good place." Riven frowned.

"Mercenaries are here." She closed her eyes and took a deep breath. "They found me the first time. Don't lose me."

~

Orlin set his mug of ale on the table as he watched the pair of arrivals search for an empty table. It was the girl and another man, not the prince. He'd always heard the princes had red hair like their father. Not that he'd ever seen any of them. This one's hair was black. His skin pale like someone who lived most of his life underground. Orlin slapped his mate.

"What'cha do that for?" he growled as the buxom woman turned away.

"We have work tonight. Come back later to play."

"What work?"

"We have a pair of travelers to take into the Dark Realm."

The pair ate a light meal hunched over, without removing their cloaks. Orlin kept his eye on them and nudged his acquaintance when they moved to leave. "Send Havish and Lem through the back. We'll box them in." Orlin left a coin with the barman and followed a few feet behind his marks. The wagon was in the alley. No one watched. He grinned. Wouldn't matter if they did.

"Hello, pretty," he said as he stepped up beside the girl and nudged her as she turned. She fell into the man. Before they could say a word, or scream, he clobbered her with a short club. The man reached for Orlin, but one of the others stepped behind and knocked him on the head as well. They dragged them both to the wagon.

~

Estellyn woke with a groan. "Riven?" Why had they taken him as well?

His dark eyes stared at her. "We are on a wide road to the Dark Realm."

"He's seeking you as well," Estellyn suddenly realized what they missed.

"This is not good."

She took his hand. "Remember what I told you. You have the light of the Maker in you. Memories of your true self."

"If he knows I am not going to turn, he will kill me."

"You'll have to convince him otherwise."

They sat silent as the wagon rolled. Estellyn came up with a plan. "It is dangerous, but Jeremian and Julsi will have the time they need to get to the pools."

Riven rubbed his face. "I don't know if I can."

"Even if we die, as long as Silverlight destroys the pools, the people of Overworld will be saved." Saying the words overwhelmed her. She did not want to die.

~

Their entrance into the Dark Realm looked like a shadow in the rock caused by surrounding trees.

Jeremian gulped. "This can't be the place."

Julsi leaned forward, wrapping her arms as best she could around Silverlight. "It is. Hold on."

With one arm around Julsi, he pressed his head against the dragon and squeezed his eyes shut. His stomach flopped as the dragon swooped. There was a rush of air, and then the light around them changed. When he opened his eyes, they were inside a cave. Silverlight landed on the ground.

"How did you find this?" Jeremian stood beside Julsi, staring up at the crack of sky through which they'd come.

"I searched for light. Couldn't reach it when I found it, but I never forgot."

"So now you're going to seek for the warrior pools?"

"What can we know of all the deep places of the world? I'm familiar with the mines, we'll want to keep away from those areas. There are other paths that lead down."

"Will Silverlight fit through them?"

Julsi tilted her head as she pondered the dragon curled up on rocks. "That hole wasn't very large, yet he got us and him through it."

Julsi waited until there was little risk of running into the miners. Fear made her hands shake. Jeremian gripped her shoulder reassuringly. "Courage is going even knowing you have reason to fear."

His words and his touch helped her take the next step.

Thirty

"It's not the prince," Orlin said as he had Riven dragged from the wagon first.

Riven fell to his knees. When he looked up, Morgeth stood before him.

"Have you done well, my servant?" Morgeth asked as Orlin dragged Estellyn from the wagon. His slow smile froze something within Riven. "You brought her, just as I asked."

"He is not yours anymore," Estellyn sneered.

Morgeth smirked. "We will see." He turned to Orlin. "Take them to the gathering hall."

Though the Elf did not go with them, Riven felt darkness pressing in on him. "I shouldn't have come with you."

Estellyn grabbed hold of his arm. "You are no longer of this dark place."

Riven shook her off. "I was a fool to think I could return and not be affected."

"You were here before. You saved my life."

Riven shook his head. "He knows I am here now. His thoughts are bent on me."

"Don't listen. Refuse him."

But Riven pulled away. "Go. Forget this madness. There is no hope for us here." His dark eyes gleamed with something Estellyn didn't understand. He stood for a moment as a tormented man, then with a curse, he turned from her and disappeared into the shadows.

"Riven," she cried after him, then cursed herself for her foolishness.

Orlin pushed Estellyn to her knees. "Go after him," he snarled at Havish.

"There is no need." Morgeth appeared from shadows. "He will come when I summon him." He walked around Estellyn. "You are much trouble. Where is the prince?"

Estellyn blinked. "Why would I know that?"

"You travelled together. I do not imagine he is far."

She narrowed her eyes. "Do you think I'd have gone to a place like Runce if the prince stayed with me? He ran home the instant he heard what you did to his brothers."

Morgeth was quiet for a moment, then smiled. "I think not. Brocahn," he raised his voice.

A tall, thick man stepped forward. "Yes, my lord?"

"Prince Jeremian is here. Find him. Take him to the pools and relieve him of his head."

"No, he's not here," Estellyn said as she jumped to her feet.

Morgeth hit her. "You do not lie well. You might even join him once I discover the truth about your nature."

Estellyn staggered back but did not fall. Orlin grabbed hold of her arms. She struggled but could only watch as Brocahn went in search of the others.

~

"I hear water," Julsi stopped with her hand on Silverlight's neck.

Jeremian looked around, but he was completely lost. "I don't know what I hear."

"This way." She led them down an incline

Jeremian could feel a breeze flow past them. "Something is here."

Silverlight gurgled.

"I don't like the smell either." She glanced at Jeremian. "It smells of death."

The downward tunnel opened into a great space. Though this cavern was dim, they could see a beach and water lapping against it.

"It's an underground lake," Julsi exclaimed.

Jeremian wasn't listening. Mounds lay on the sand. It took a moment to recognize clothes. To realize there were bodies. He sat hard and stared. The short body of Edmund was easy to recognize, even without his head. Aeol wore his cloak of the kingship, though his hands were bound behind him. Four others. He closed his eyes and spoke their names. "Orlith, Snechtal, Lindulf, and Duncan."

"I'm so sorry," Julsi dropped beside him. Scuffling noises in the tunnel alerted her. "Someone is coming."

Jeremian shook himself. "You must not be found." He searched wildly. "How do you hide a dragon?"

"There may be another tunnel further in."

Jeremian stood, his face grim. "Go. Find a place to hide." He took a breath and grabbed her hand. "Destroying the pools is more important than me. Wait for the right moment." He pushed her away then faced the tunnel. Even he could hear someone approach.

~

"What is that name they gave him? Riven?" Morgeth asked, watching Estellyn. "You have such hope for him." His eyes narrowed. "Yet, there is doubt. Do you realize that, Riven?"

"I don't know what I am." Riven stepped forward.

Morgeth's smile chilled Estellyn. "Of course, you do." He beckoned Riven to come closer. "This dark place holds more for you than Overworld ever could."

"You speak lies." Estellyn pulled away from Orlin.

Morgeth drew Riven close enough to grasp one side of his face. "Do I lie to you?"

Estellyn watched pain flicker through Riven's features. His eyes hardened.

Morgeth stepped back. "Your request sent you to Overworld. Your desire to consume her drove you to find her. Her nature may be enticing, but it is not who you are. Don't you think it time to reveal your true self to her?"

"Riven, don't do this," Estellyn begged as his foul breath wafted across her face.

He leaned in. "Did you think you could change the nature of things?" His voice hissed. "I warned you what returning to this place would do to me."

Laughter rose from the Dark Lord. "Did you think to contend with me? Those foolish creatures of light have misled you. They have given you over to the dark for sacrifice."

Riven backed away as Morgeth approached Estellyn. His touch on her cheek was cold. "You are beauty and light." His voice softened.

Estellyn felt trapped in his blue eyes. His thoughts probed her mind, but she could not break away.

"So much goodness." His lip twisted. "So much

hope." He grabbed a handful of her hair and pulled her close. "We can change that. It's what I do best." He shoved her away.

She fell against Riven. His hand dug into her shoulder.

He gazed on them both and breathed a harsh smile. "Break her."

Riven knocked her to the ground. The air around them seemed to shiver with the excitement of those watching. He pulled a thick stick from beneath his robes and struck her. She rolled from the force, pain radiating through her shoulder. He held the stick with one hand and leaned over to pull her to her feet. She struggled against his grip but could not release herself. He wrapped his arm around her and dragged her against him.

"Riven!" She fought him.

His countenance darkened. "It's time."

Estellyn grabbed the staff. Riven struck Morgeth, knocking his former master to the ground. Estellyn lifted the staff into the air then slammed it down on black stone. Light poured into the Dark Realm. Creatures giggling with glee suddenly screamed in terror and agony. Their twisted bodies scrambled out of the great hall desperate for shadows to hide them. Morgeth stood against the light, though the white of his face burned. "Light will not avail you for long."

Estellyn trembled. "Only long enough to destroy the works of your hands."

Somewhere within the system of caves that formed the Dark Realm, a dragon roared. The earth shook with its power.

~

Jeremian closed his eyes against the sight of oily

pools of water, against the sight of his six brothers, headless, lying with their blood spilled across the sand and water. He breathed, holding himself as straight as he could, even though they'd forced him to his knees where cold water lapped against him. He felt the press of a blade against the back of his neck as they lined up to strike. Fear and flight urged him to beg and whimper, but he held himself still with the steel of his royal blood.

Julsi reached for a stone. With all the force she could muster, she ran from her hiding place and launched the stone at the man with the sword. Two things happened. The man staggered back at the blow, dropping his sword which clanked on the rock. Then light blazed through the water caverns before fading away.

Julsi grabbed Jeremian, helping him to his feet. "Silverlight, now," she cried as they ran. The wall seemed to shift. Silver light streamed through a body. The dragon opened his eyes. Julsi stopped with a gasp, turning to look. Jeremian, hands still bound behind him, leaned against her. They saw dark gloomy pools spreading like lakes as far as could be seen. The image in her mind showed bodies of growing warriors, fed on the blood of Jeremian's brothers. Their thickening bodies battled beneath the oily surface of the water. Silverlight roared. Julsi stumbled at the trembling of the ground beneath her feet. She wrapped an arm around Jeremian and ran as the room behind them lit with dragon fire. The roar of the firestorm swallowed up screams of those it devoured.

Thirty-One

Riven crumpled to the floor at a blow from Morgeth. The Dark Lord's eyes gleamed with cold and dark as he stared at Estellyn. "You think you can destroy me?"

She tightened her grip on the staff. "Maybe not destroy. To leave you cowering in your hole a while longer suits me."

"Is that what you think? A dragon has awoken. Your light won't stand against it. I will burn your world until the very sun is blotted out for a generation."

"The dragon isn't yours." Estellyn held out the staff pointing at the wall. An image appeared. Silver flames flew from the mouth of a dragon across a wide expanse of water. Water boiled from its heat. Things stretched up, trying to escape the hungry flames, but they were consumed. The fire spread across the vastness until it licked stone that hadn't been touched in millennia. Thick smoke rolled through the cavern.

Morgeth screamed with fury. He lunged at Estellyn, drawing out a slender dagger. Riven grabbed his ankle, yanking hard. Morgeth fell on his dagger. In the waning light, Estellyn watched blood spread beneath him. She blinked, shook herself, then grabbed hold of Riven to pull him to his feet. Though they ran, she couldn't keep herself from looking back. "Is he dead?"

Riven shook his head. "The body is merely a house. Whatever Morgeth is will find its way to a new house."

They turned a corner then gasped. Starlight came toward them. "You should not be here," Estellyn hurried to her side.

The unicorn pranced, shaking its head.

Estellyn shuddered. "Not even for our sake. The darkness here is not stayed."

"Get on," Riven ordered as a shapeless form of dark gathered from the fallen body of Morgeth.

Estellyn obeyed. Riven joined her and Starlight galloped forward. The darkness spread behind them. Air frosted. Starlight fought against the weight of it, but Estellyn could feel her muscles quivering.

"We won't make the exit," Riven's deep voice spoke what her heart feared.

"We have to."

Riven leaned close. "Don't let her go, Starlight. Don't allow her to follow me."

Estellyn gasped "What do you mean? What are you doing?"

"It won't stop him, but you'll have enough time to make the surface. Then fly, as far from this realm as you can."

"Riven, no," she grabbed hold of his shirt.

"I have to." His eyes glittered for a moment. "I love you."

His unexpected kiss took her breath, and then he was gone. She twisted but could see nothing in the growing dark. "Riven!" Her scream was swallowed by the formless mass. She tried to fall back, but Starlight held her tight with her wings. "We can't leave him," she cried, struggling.

The air rent with a scream, long and cold, like a waning cry of battle. Estellyn's throat choked with the sound. The shadow faded and Starlight leapt ahead with her own cry. Estellyn bowed her head to the unicorn's back. Grief overwhelmed her. Not even the touch of sunlight eased the pain.

Starlight raced into the woods. Trees flashed as she carried them away from the Dark Realm.

Estellyn slept. Starlight's movement to drink woke her. She sat up with a frown. The moon glowed overhead, causing tiny white flowers across the glen to shine with light. She slid from the back of the unicorn, staggering on wobbly legs. "This is the same place I first met your mother and Lystra. Are we safe?"

Starlight shook her head up and down then started grazing on the flowers. Estellyn walked to regain feeling in her legs. A silver gown lay on a rock beside the deep pool. She glanced around, but there was no one else. An image of herself, tunic stained with dirt and blood came to mind. She furrowed her brows but looked at her reflection in the water. There was no doubt she'd been in a battle of sorts. "Fine." She crouched to touch the water. Expecting it to be cold, the warmth flowing over her hand felt good. "If someone had mentioned this was a heated pool, I'd have bathed here long ago."

Without soap there was only so much she could do, but she felt clean and refreshed, dressing in the silver gown. Tiredness weighed on her. What had happened to Riven? To Jeremian and Julsi? She made a bed beneath an old tree. She was too worn to do more that curl up and hope the new day would prove their plan had not failed.

~

"Wait, your binds," Julsi paused to pick up a sharp rock. It didn't take long for her to cut Jeremian's hands free. They jogged through the hallway, across a bridge, and into tunnels.

"Where are we going?"

"A way out that Silverlight can follow." She turned to look down a corridor and stopped. "That's Riven," she gasped when she saw a body strewn on the floor.

Jeremian grabbed her arm. "Be cautious. He shouldn't be alone."

Though they paused, nothing moved. She worried her bottom lip. "Do you think he's alive?"

"I don't know. Even if he is, should we trust him?"

Julsi looked at Jeremian as she covered his hand with her own. "Estellyn trusts him. Do you trust her?"

"Yes."

His quick response did not surprise her. "We help him. Come on."

Riven wasn't dead, neither was he coherent. They carried him between them, looping his arms over their shoulders.

"Which way?" Jeremian asked.

Julsi led them further along the tunnel. "These marks are from hooves. The unicorn must have escaped."

"With Estellyn, I hope. But why leave Riven?"

A chirp sounded somewhere behind them. Julsi made him stop so she could turn and whistle. Chirping sounded closer and darts of silver splashed along the walls.

Jeremian pressed his free hand against the wall of the tunnel. "This best not get any narrower. We should keep going."

"I want to be certain he's safe."

Riven moaned, but still Julsi refused to move until Silverlight came into view. He kept his body low but could walk. Julsi grinned.

"Now can we go?" Jeremian chuckled, but he didn't mind having a dragon at their back during the long climb to the surface.

They came out in a large cave leading into forest. Trees and sunlight washed the gloom of the Dark Realm from their faces. Once they reached sunlight, they lay Riven on the ground. He moaned again, shifting his head.

Jeremian pressed his hand against silvery-brown bark. "I didn't think I'd see a tree again."

Julsi greeted Silverlight by rubbing her hands against the side of his head. "Have we stopped him? Has Morgeth been stayed?"

"For now, at least, thanks to Silverlight." Jeremian stared at the dragon. "It seemed as though I could see the waters burning. Whatever was in them have been destroyed."

"I'm sorry about your brothers."

"I don't understand how it could happen. How all of them were taken." He frowned toward Riven. "He was the only servant of Morgeth I knew."

"We should get you home."

He shook his head. "Not until we find Estellyn. She's alone."

Julsi nodded, ignoring the tightness in her throat. Silverlight bumped her shoulder and chirped.

Jeremian swallowed. "What's he thinking?"

"He can carry the three of us so we can find her."

"Are you sure?" He faced the dragon. "I don't want

you overburdened. Find a safe haven for them and come back and get me."

That made Julsi laugh. "To think you hated dragons only a few days ago."

"I was wrong, I admit it. How do we do this?"

Riven lay between them. Silverlight's wings beat the air with strength, and they lifted into the sky. Julsi felt her stomach swirl, but she kept her eyes open. They could see nothing beneath the cover of trees.

"Where would she go?" Julsi shouted above the roar of wind.

"If she's on Starlight, would she go to the glen in the Highland Ridges? Astebery may be waiting for her foal." Even though he couldn't explain how to get there, Silverlight only needed the images from his mind. With a tilt of a wing, they turned northward.

They stopped at an abandoned farm before twilight. "How is he?" Julsi leaned over Jeremian to watch Riven.

"Breathing, but he hasn't woken up."

"I know nothing of medicine." She wiggled her foot. "It was crushed by a rock, and they did nothing. I walked with a limp until the dragon healed me."

"Healed you?"

She shrugged. "It's straight. The bones are strong."

"Can he help Riven?"

"I think he would have if he could."

"I'm going to look for food, and possibly something to make into beds. Are you okay staying with him?"

Julsi blinked. She'd rather go with Jeremian, but Riven needed watching. "Of course, I'll stay."

He returned with a basket of dried fruit, bread, and

a chunk of meat. Riven remained as he was. Silverlight ate hay stored in the back room. Stars gleamed outside of their shelter. "Must be different from the world you knew below." Jeremian spread a rough blanket across her shoulders.

"I feel small, as though a slight wind will carry me away."

"Do you remember anything before… well, from when you were little?"

"I remember running along a broken path trying to get this thing attached to a string to go up in the air. Then there were fires in the night, flames and screams." She closed her eyes with a shiver.

Jeremian placed a hand on her shoulder. "I'm sorry, I shouldn't ask you to think about those memories."

"I don't know what happened to any of them."

"I remember horrible raids about fifteen years ago. Father said those who died on the surface were better off than the survivors taken to the Dark Realm. He never imagined villagers like you with strength and courage to defy Morgeth."

Her cheeks warmed. "I'm not sure about strength and courage. I wanted a place to die peacefully."

He tilted his head. "Die? Or were you searching for freedom?"

"Death was the only course of freedom I could imagine. I know better now." She looked at him, wanting to say more, but knowing her place. "I'm tired."

"There's a hay bed near Silverlight. Don't let the shadows from today mar your dreams."

She placed her hand on his arm and left him facing the night sky.

Thirty-Two

She remembered no dreams, though her mind felt foggy. Jeremian seemed no better. They flew in silence, Riven still unconscious between them. Forests gave way to fields with rivers running through them. They skirted villages and areas where people might look up and spy the dragon sweeping overhead. Mountains in the distance drew closer. Afternoon was waning when they finally reached their destination.

Jeremian pointed at a field. "Land there. We can walk the rest of the way. It won't be far."

Her legs were shaky as she stood. They pulled Riven from the dragon, holding him between them once more. Julsi huffed to get hair out of her face. "Where do we go from here?"

Jeremian looked around then tilted his head. "That way. It will be a little rough."

"We can always let Silverlight go first, clear a path for us."

He grunted. "How about Silverlight rests here. You can call him if he is needed."

The dragon munched on fresh grass. Julsi let Jeremian lead. Crawling through uneven brush was like having to walk the rock falls. "Now would be a good time to wake and help, friend," Jeremian muttered.

Julsi agreed as they pulled Riven along with them. "Where is this place? I thought you said near."

"Through here. I think this is it." They followed a creek. The path became evident, evening out and free of obstacles. They followed it into the glen. "Estellyn," Jeremian cried out as she jumped to her feet.

~

Her face lit with a smile as she moved closer. Until she hesitated. "Where did you find him? Why have you brought him here?" Estellyn shivered as they leaned Riven against a tree. "Is he alive?"

"Yes," Jeremian frowned. "But badly wounded. He hasn't woken since we found him in a tunnel."

"Why did you leave him?" Julsi asked with her hands on her hips.

Estellyn shook her head. "I didn't. He sacrificed himself so we could escape."

"From what? Morgeth wouldn't have left him lying there."

"Morgeth is dead. At least, the body he used died. The master of the deep is indeed a darkness, without form."

"You provided one for me." Riven stood, stretching. He smiled at the dumb looks from Jeremian and Julsi.

Estellyn fought against her emotions. This wasn't the same man who'd talked of love. "Why are you here? You'd be safer in your Dark Realm."

He moved a step closer. "Don't be foolish enough to think light will destroy me. Granted, I work best in the shadows of night," he held up his hand, "but this is not going to destroy me."

"Perhaps not." Jeremian pulled Julsi behind him as Riven walked in their direction.

Riven laughed. "Fear me now? Why? You helped me when I was hurt. You are my friends."

"I'm not sure you were as hurt as you seemed," Jeremian touched his side but there was no weapon.

Riven laughed again. "Nothing to protect yourselves with? How foolish."

"Leave them be." Estellyn stood straight. "You are here, drawn out from your underworld. Why is that? Or has Riven somehow managed to influence you?"

"A slave, influence me? Ludicrous. If you saw what he truly was, you would never have befriended him."

"You could not be defeated in your realm, but what can protect you here?"

He sneered, "I see no threats."

Estellyn motioned with her head. "Not us. Behind you."

While they'd been talking, the unicorns had gathered. Starlight gleamed beside her mother, Astebery. The stallion stood with them. Riven showed the first sign of concern, although he covered it quickly. "I spent two days whispering to a dragon. At my beckoning, this haven, this entire mountainside, will burn."

~

Julsi gasped, pulling from Jeremian. "Silverlight!" She ran before Jeremian could stop her.

Returning to the field where they'd left the dragon went much faster without the burden of carrying a traitor. Silverlight sat among the grass, his tail twitching.

"Are you alright?" She stopped when his eyes

landed on her. "I didn't know he wasn't who we thought. Don't let him spoil you. You were meant to help us."

Images of the burning filled her mind, making her want to gag. She pushed them away. With eyes closed tight, she thought about finding him, wrapping him close to her to keep him warm.

A roar shook the air, making her fall to her feet.

~

"Any hold you have on the dragon will be weak," Jeremian spoke.

Riven laughed. "What does a King's son know about dragons?" The sound of dragon roar widened his smile. "Perhaps your friend has become its first sacrifice?"

Estellyn tightened her grip on the staff. "Enough. Depart his body and be gone."

The unicorn entered the glen.

Riven sneered. "The Maker's guard? You have come to be destroyed."

At the stallion's snort, Estellyn and Jeremian backed away. Air shimmered. Sight of the animals faded, and three beings stood. Their brightness seemed greater than the sun. It was impossible to see what manner of persons they were. Each carried a golden sword. They surrounded Riven.

"Your time has ended." Their voices spoke as hundreds.

Riven growled but could not speak against them.

"While we could not enter the Dark Realm without fear of death, you have divided yourself and come to us." Their words whispered.

Estellyn and Jeremian fell to their knees, shielding their faces. The three raised their swords high above

Riven. They seemed to move as shadows of the unicorns raced around in a circle. Though no sound came from the storm brewing where the blades touched, air whipped. Vibrant energy raged. Estellyn felt as though she could get swept away with it.

Darkness withdrew from Riven like a black mist. It formed a sphere, twisting to make a way past the blades, but the creatures held it. The black mass curled around itself, thicker and darker, yet could not break free. The mountain seemed to scream. Air exploded. The force of it knocked Estellyn backward as it stole her breath. The black mist gathered into a single point, then with the touch of the blades, it disappeared forever.

Thirty-Three

For a moment Estellyn felt she would never be able to breathe again. In her panic she forgot how. But then the panic passed. Air flowed over her. Brilliance faded. She dared open her eyes. Three unicorns contentedly munched on grass and clover. She rolled to her side. Her hands shook, but she grasped the staff to pull herself to her feet. Her legs weren't steady. Jeremian didn't bother to stand. He crawled the short distance and turned Riven over.

Estellyn covered her mouth to hold in a sob. He was deathly pale with blood smeared across the side of his face. Starlight moved closer to them. She gulped. "Was that you?"

"As a letter written by you remains part of yourself," Lystra said, drawing near. "Their spirits remain close to the Maker." She glanced down at Riven. "He could not deny the nature that molded him."

Estellyn shook her head. "He does not belong to the dark. He was like Julsi, taken as a child. He started as a slave. Twisted over time, yes, but in the end, he remembered his true nature."

"Can they do that? Look how he betrayed you."

Estellyn crouched and used her sleeve to wipe blood from his face. "He didn't betray us. He purposed to go into the shadow, knowing what it could do to him." She took hold of his hand. "His actions provided the moments we needed to escape." She glanced at Lystra. "Even possessed, he somehow caused Morgeth to leave the Dark Realm, to come where he could be destroyed once and for all."

Lystra tilted her head. "These things I didn't know."

"Can he be saved?"

Jeremian shook his head. "He's been possessed by the spirit of darkness. The peace of death may be preferred to those memories."

Lystra didn't seem convinced. "Why would he sacrifice himself?"

"For love." Riven breathed. "Just please chop my bloody head off if there is to be any more of this." He didn't open his eyes, but his grin filled Estellyn with joy.

~

Silverlight lowered his head and chirped. Julsi felt tears burn her eyes. "Many will fear you. Evil ones will try to turn you to their purpose. I don't know if there are more like Riven."

The dragon sang a long note as its wings twitched. She blinked. "If you fly high enough, you'll see empty places, wide fields and tall mountains. You can make your home there. Come and see me when you want." Her voice broke.

Silverlight rubbed his head against her shoulder then lifted into the air, spiraling skyward. He opened his wings and the wind carried him away. Julsi stared until even the spec of him disappeared. Something caused the mountain to shake. She ran back to the glen.

~

"We should return to the inn, the one with your admirer." Jeremian spoke quietly, even as he teased.

"Julsi can stay with me," Estellyn glanced at the younger woman, who nodded. "Give Riven time to heal."

"Again." Jeremian's grin lasted a moment, before his features darkened, and he looked away.

Estellyn placed her hand on his arm. "You should return to Allington. Your parents need you."

He closed his eyes. "Not yet. I am the seventh son. There is nothing remarkable in me."

"Astebery thought differently." She touched the white strands of his hair.

Rather than acknowledge her, he waved at Julsi and Riven. "How will we carry him?"

Lystra joined them. "A wagon and horse await you on the road. It will not move fast as the unicorn, but one should not expect to ride on the back of a unicorn often."

Estellyn smiled as she watched Astebery and Starlight. "What will they do now? Will they disappear? Is there a different place for them to go?"

Lystra sat on the grass beside Estellyn and Jeremian. "I do not know what they will do. There is much for us yet to learn."

They sat in companionable silence for a time until Estellyn stretched and stood. "We should go if we want to arrive before dark." She turned to Lystra. "Will we meet again?"

"I think we must, though I do not know by what circumstance."

I hope someday to learn more about my people,"

Estellyn said as she moved the hair near her ear.

Jeremian frowned but said nothing.

Lystra handed him a satchel of food. "Enough for the day," she explained. "May the Maker guide your way."

"Thank you." A more elegant response did not come to mind. He sighed.

Estellyn squeezed his arm before crossing to Julsi and Riven.

~

With the uneventful ride behind them, Jeremian waited at the bar in the common room for a couple of drinks. Not many people were there. Those who were had no knowledge of what had transpired. No knowledge that one day he would be their king. The thought made him choke. Were they happy? Someone sneezed. He glanced in that direction. Were they healthy? What did he know about being to them what they needed him to be?

"You still want your cider?" The bartender interrupted his wayward thoughts.

Jeremian offered a tight smile and picked up the mugs, then turned toward the table with his friends. Julsi kept watch through one of the windows.

"You miss the dragon?" Jeremian asked as he placed a mug of warmed cider on the table.

She sighed. "Strange, isn't it?"

He sat across from her with another mug. She lifted hers. Jeremian tapped it with his. "That means cheers. It's a way of saying what you did mattered."

She sipped. "It tastes like something I almost remember."

"Apples. I had them add hot water. I know you

aren't able to abide strong flavors."

Her cheeks warmed. "Thank you." After a moment of silence, she peeked at him. "What will you do now? Return home?"

His shoulders tightened. "I need to, yes, but I'm tempted to stay away. I never expected to be next in line for the throne."

"You've flown on a dragon; you'll grow into a good leader."

He chuckled. "Guess if I have problems with enemies, I can have you contact Silverlight."

Her mug hit the table. "Do you think I could?"

"There's a bond that connects you. I think it connects all of us." He smiled. "Return with me to the castle."

"Me?" Julsi stared at him, her green eyes dazzling like light in a gem.

"You have no family, remember? Let us be there for you."

She looked down. "Wouldn't you rather Estellyn go with you?"

He laughed. "She won't."

"Then why not stay with her?"

He took a drink. "The palace is where I'm needed. My offer is for you. I want you to come." Not certain as to why, Jeremian was pleased when she nodded. His parents would be hurting from the loss of his brothers. Julsi could use them for care as much as they could use her for comfort.

Estellyn joined them a few moments later. "Is he sleeping?" She asked Jeremian.

"Yes. He's recovering. Should be able to return him to the castle guard in a few days."

Julsi leaned forward, her eyes wide. "Is he in trouble?"

"Of course not," Jeremian shook his head. "He works with the training officers to prepare our soldiers." Something within his chest tightened and he frowned. "You can be certain I will speed up the training process and strengthen our military."

Julsi meant to take a drink but lowered her mug as she glanced out the window. "You don't think trouble from the Dark Realm is over?"

"Someone betrayed us, but we don't know who. Lord Morgeth may be defeated, but the Dark Realm still exists. How do we know evil will not soon rise again?"

Estellyn grabbed hold of his hand. "I am sorry it has fallen to you to think of such things."

"How soon do you return to your family?" Julsi asked.

Estellyn smiled as she let Jeremian go. "I should leave tomorrow." She took a drink. "What of you? Do you want to come with me?"

Julsi looked at Jeremian, then bent her head.

"I thought she should come with me." Jeremian explained. "She may bring comfort."

Estellyn nodded. "Allington has many knowledgeable people for council. Perhaps they will share what happened to your family."

Jeremian lifted his mug. "To new friends and unknown futures."

The sound of their mugs clinking seemed a closing on their adventure.

Thirty-Four

Estellyn returned to the glen on a sunny afternoon a few days later. Riven, Jeremian, and Julsi sent word they were heading to Allington by horseback. The adventure *had* ended. She'd found more than expected, and yet her heart remained unsettled. "Why is that?" She asked aloud although no one else was there. She sat on the grass enjoying the feel of sunlight on her shoulders. She laid the staff on the ground beside her. "There's more. I know there's more, I just don't know what it is." Her voice carried away, unanswered. In her heart she knew it wouldn't always be silent.

LAURIE LEE

224

About the Author:

Laurie Lee is a fantasy novelist penname for Laurie Boulden. Laurie lives in Central Florida where summer seems to reign supreme. She teaches at Warner University, whose goal is to graduate students with a love for Christ and longing to promote the Kingdom of God. Teaching for twenty-six years has given her plenty of fodder for creating stories. When she isn't working or writing, she lives close to her mother, so they are able to spend quality time together.

Writing has been a passion since childhood. In college, she learned about photography and has been smitten ever since. Through the influence of her father, she also loves to travel. She loves to explore new places and uses nature to drive her creative spirit. You can see some of Laurie's pictures on her website: www.laurieleefairyland.com. Sign up for her newsletter, and you'll see even more.

Books by Laurie Lee:

Books by Laurie Boulden
Please click on a picture for the link

Laurie Boulden
Cookies,
Cocoa, and
Capers

HIDDEN
GEMS
LAURIE BOULDEN